YEARN

HELLISH #7

CHARITY PARKERSON

Punk & Sissy

--Warning: This book is intended for readers over the age of 18.

Copyright © 2018 Charity Parkerson
Editor: BZ Hercules & Consultants
ISBN-13: 978-1-946099-41-9
All rights reserved.

INTRODUCTION

A CURSED TIGER. A SEXY COP. NOTHING IN COMMON EXCEPT A POWERFUL ATTRACTION.

It's been months since Saber was cursed by Baptiste for his mistakes with Evan. With no relief in sight, and his pride stopping him from begging for forgiveness, he's had to get his adrenaline rushes elsewhere. It's a move that's landed him in the sights of a super sexy cop.

Saber Khatri is the opposite of everything Landry stands for in life. The huge blond is wild, reckless, cocky, and—Landry suspects—deadly. Landry knows Saber is keeping secrets from him. What Landry doesn't realize is that his inability to resist Saber's killer good looks might literally be the death of him.

ONE

THE WIND WHIPPED AT SABER'S HAIR. HIS senses were on high alert as he weaved between cars. He saw everything. Felt everything. As a weretiger, he was a wild animal at heart. It went against his nature to be docile. He needed freedom. Adrenaline. A slight vibration ran through his arms and between his thighs as he pushed his bike to the limits. Cars blew their horns as he made space between them while never letting off the gas. One hundred. One-ten. Saber's pulse beat in his ears as he reached one-twenty. He needed the rush. There was nothing else in his life. No ties. If he crashed, it might kill him if he didn't heal quickly enough. No one would miss him. He didn't care.

Life had been complete shit since Baptiste cursed him. As much as Saber recognized he shouldn't have fucked with Baptiste's wolf, the punishment did not fit the crime. There was no avoiding his wild streak. The animal inside always won. When he'd tugged Evan into a closet during a party at Riskel's, something odd happened. The scent of purity overcame him. He'd been hard as a rock, even though some blonde chick had just blown him not two minutes earlier. What was that girl's name? He'd seen her once more afterward. Funny. He'd seen Evan again that night as well. Damn, short attention span. He couldn't focus on one thing. One person. Evan had him hard with his pure scent and there was something about that he'd never admitted to anyone. Another man had never made him hard. Now, thanks to Baptiste's curse, nothing did.

In his world, there wasn't such a thing as sexuality. Mates were chosen by Goddess Celeste. Until then, everyone was free to fuck whoever got their rocks off. As animals, the genitalia attached never factored into the equation. It was the moon. The alignment of the stars. A scent on the air. Evan's scent had done it. In truth, though, he scared Saber a little. Evan was a wolf of honor and position. Saber was a nobody who got invited to the party because of a loose connection to a pack. Still, Saber hadn't been able to resist inviting Evan to his cabin. He'd shown more self-control with Evan than ever before. They hadn't fucked. A smile curved Saber's lips. They'd done everything else. No one had walked away unsatisfied. Saber's smile fell. He should've stayed away. That one day of stolen passion had cost him dearly.

Saber focused harder on pushing the bike. He hit one-forty. The adrenaline wasn't enough to wipe the bleakness from his brain. He needed more. Saber couldn't be honest with anyone. Still, the truth wouldn't leave him alone. What he needed was to fuck, but he didn't want just anyone anymore. He wanted Evan. The bike slowed a hair as he let the truth into his heart. He wanted Evan, but he'd fucked up. The way he always did. Now Evan had a mate. Wolves mated for life. Saber had lost his chance. Blue lights flashed behind him. A loud curse rang through his helmet. For a moment, he considered not stopping. They probably wouldn't catch him. He couldn't end up on the news. With a growl, Saber slowed. Exposing his kind to humans came with a harsher punishment than jail. There wasn't a chance in hell he could outrun the gods who controlled them. He eased to the shoulder of the road and parked before taking off his helmet.

"Step off the bike. Walk backward toward me with your hands in the air." The instructions came from the patrol car's loud speaker. Saber did as told, walking backward. "Get on your knees, lie face down, and put your hands behind your back."

Saber glanced down at his white shirt and sighed before following the cop's instructions. The pavement was hot as hell. He half expected a knee to the back and rough treatment any second. Saber stayed still, hoping they understood he wouldn't fight. A shadow fell over him. That was all the warning he had before cold cuffs snapped around his wrists.

"Do you have any weapons, drugs, or needles? Let me know now. Don't let me find them first."

"No, sir."

The cop bore Saber's weight as he tugged him upward. That move impressed Saber. Even though he looked human, Saber wasn't. His muscle weighed more. "Get a knee underneath you and I'll keep you from falling over."

Saber followed every instruction until he was on

his feet. To his surprise, once he was upright, he was nose to nose with the dude. That was rare. Humans almost never met his height. His eyes were blue. Saber shouldn't have noticed, but they were a crazy shade of blue—like the waters of Havelock Island in India. Saber hadn't seen his home in over one hundred years. He was looking at it now in a stranger's eyes.

"Where's your wallet?"

Saber blinked at the question, wiping away his traveling thoughts. "Right back pocket."

"I'm not going to get stuck by a needle or anything, right?"

"There's nothing in my pockets but keys, a phone, and my wallet."

With a sharp nod, the guy patted him down, pulling out the keys, phone, and wallet. "I'll hold your arm while you sit. We're going to be here a minute."

Saber nodded and slowly dropped to his ass on the ground.

Obviously satisfied Saber would cooperate, the guy flipped open Saber's wallet and inspected Saber's ID. "Saber Khatri. Where are you from originally, Mr. Khatri?"

"India," Saber answered honestly.

The cop eyed him. Saber knew what he was seeing. Blond hair. Light blue eyes. Not the typical coloration for his country, but he was typical for a tiger. "Do they let you drive one-thirty-five on a busy interstate in India, endangering innocent lives and risking your life in the process?"

Saber fought a smile. "No, sir."

He flipped Saber's wallet closed. For a moment, he stared at Saber as if trying to decide what to do with him. Saber stared back, staying compliant. The dude was perfectly built—like carved from marble. Every muscle was well-defined, even the ones in his jaw. His dark hair was at odds with his crazy blue eyes and tanned skin. Saber's gaze dropped to his name tag—LaTour. Saber assumed that was his last name. A native New Orleans man.

"Do you have any outstanding warrants?"

"No, sir."

"Have you been drinking?"

Saber wished he could get drunk. "No, sir."

LaTour nodded. "Come on. Let's move you to a shady spot and get out of the sun while we figure this out." He pulled Saber to his feet and walked him to passenger side of his patrol car, where they were out of danger on the side of the road and in the shade. Once again, he helped Saber to sit on the ground. "That's better. Now how about you tell me why I clocked you doing over one-twenty on this fine day?"

Saber fought another smile. He didn't miss the fact that the guy had dropped his speed a hair. That speed wouldn't get him any less arrested, but the fine would go down. "Just blowing off steam and not watching my speed."

LaTour smiled. It was a breathtaking sight—dimples and perfect teeth. Saber noticed its beauty in a detached sort of way. "You didn't see all the cars you were cutting off?"

"I thought everyone seemed to be out for a Sunday drive today."

LaTour's smile brightened. "Except it's Tuesday."

Saber nodded, staying serious, even though he wanted to laugh. "In New Orleans, that's a lazy day."

The radio LaTour wore crackled before a voice filtered out. "Car 410, I have the information on that 505. 2016 Harley Iron 883. Registered owner Saber Khatri of 111 Redwood Lane, New Orleans."

LaTour pushed the button to respond. "10-4. Could I get a 10-29 with driver held?"

"10-4."

LaTour relaxed against the car. "I'm just waiting to see if you have any warrants."

Saber had known his word wouldn't be enough, so he wasn't worried. It was hot out, but he was in no hurry to get to jail.

The man crossed his arms over his chest. "So you were doing a hundred and not paying attention. Were you racing?"

This time, at the change in his speed, Saber couldn't contain his smile. Laughter sounded in his voice when he answered. "No, sir."

"That's good. These streets are dangerous enough."

The radio crackled. "Car 410. On that 10-29 for the 505. No outstanding warrants."

"10-4," LaTour responded. "Code four."

"10-4 car 410."

LaTour straightened from the car and helped Saber to his feet. This time, things didn't go as smoothly. Saber slipped, falling forward, before ending up flush against the officer. The man's scent overwhelmed him. He smelled like the jungle. Saber didn't know how else to explain it. The man was wild and untamed. He would bite and tear at the skin of anyone who tried to break him. Saber went hard. He sucked in a breath. It had been months.

Risk had been ensconced with the king and unable to make him a potion to break Baptiste's curse. But this human, yet another man, had affected him. Saber's shock was bone deep. He couldn't even blink. All he could do was hold the man's stare as lust pumped through his veins, consuming him. Then LaTour took a step back, and it was over. It was as if Saber hadn't gotten hard at all. Disappointment beat at his brain, nearly breaking him.

LaTour moved behind him and unlocked the cuffs. "If I write you a ticket for that eighty-five in a seventy zone, will you make me regret my decision?"

Saber blinked. He couldn't think straight. "No, sir. Thank you." In truth, Saber wasn't sure if he thanked the man for his kindness or for showing him his body still worked. Saber rubbed his wrists, trying to get the circulation back in his hands the moment they were free. He stood still while LaTour wrote his ticket. When he handed Saber his wallet, keys, phone, and ticket, Saber tried not to show any reaction over the massive amount. It was better than jail.

"Have a good day, Mr. Khatri. In the future, keep it reasonable."

Saber experienced an odd pang at the idea of never seeing the man again. Given the circumstances, it was beyond ridiculous, but—for a moment—Saber had been aroused. That was mind blowing. It could be that the curse was wearing off, and this guy was the first person to accidentally brush his dick in months, but still. "What's your first name?" Saber asked before he could think better of it.

He didn't answer right away. Saber glanced up from where he'd been stuffing his ticket in his wallet to avoid eye contact. LaTour watched him as if waiting to have Saber's full attention. "It's Landry."

Saber's mouth lifted in one corner. "New Orleans through and through."

Landry's eyes lit with something—like he had a secret. Saber wanted the man's thoughts. "Yep, so be more careful and don't kill anyone in my town." On that note, Landry circled the car and jumped behind the wheel. With a small shake of his head, hoping to dislodge Landry from his brain, Saber headed back to his bike. Damn, it had been a weird day.

HE WAS SUCH A DUMBASS. Landry barely stopped himself from covering his face. This was the first time in his sixteen years on the force that he'd let someone go because they were hot. No doubt Saber Khatri would make him regret the decision. His gaze wouldn't budge from Saber. That ass. The sexy, confident walk. Damn. No doubt, they'd be scraping the dumbass from the road one day. Probably today, since Landry let him go. Landry needed the dude out of his sight. It was the way Saber had looked at him when he'd stumbled, and their bodies had collided. Landry blew out a slow breath. No one had ever stared him with such intensity—like a predator.

Landry's cell phone rang, jerking him from the fantasy of what such a hard body could do to him. He checked the face. Seeing his brother's name, he answered.

"Hello?"

"Hey, baby brother. What's up?"

Landry rolled his eyes. To Shepherd, Landry would always be his baby brother, even at thirty-five. "Working. What's up with you?"

"Same. Hey, so, I'm coming to town and Frankie and I are headed out to Raff's Pool Hall tonight. Are you in?"

Saber straddled the Harley. Tight jeans stretched across his massive thighs. Landry took a breath. Any distraction was welcome. "Yeah. What time?"

"Let's meet at eight."

Landry nodded like Shepherd could see him. "I'll see you then."

Shepherd being Shepherd, he was always stupid. "Peace out, brother."

A snort escaped Landry. "Yeah. Bye." He shook his head as he disconnected their call. Saber put on his helmet, adjusting his thick, long blond hair. The muscles in his forearms flexed with every motion. Landry chewed on the side of his nail. Try as he might, Landry couldn't force himself to pull away and miss a second of the show. Damn, the way Saber's white t-shirt strained against his wide shoulders and biceps was sexy as fuck. Landry needed to get laid. That was all there was to it. Raff's was mostly a biker bar and kind of rough. It wasn't the type of place he'd find anyone, but damned if he wouldn't keep an eye out. Maybe after a few beers, he'd call Nolan. Nolan was one of those people who was always up for a no-strings-attached fuck. The idea sounded better by the second. Nolan was the exact opposite of Saber. He was slight of frame and sweet. Nothing about sex with someone like Saber would be sweet. Landry would definitely lose some skin. The longing that slammed into Landry at the thought made him glad he was sitting down. He stared at his car's onboard computer system to give his eyes something else to do besides watching Saber.

A knock sounded on the window, startling Landry. He glanced over to find Saber waiting for his attention. Landry rolled down the window. Saber leaned down and propped his arms on Landry's door. His smile looked over-the-top cocky. "I have a question before I go. Have you been to lunch?"

Surprise had Landry blinking in confusion. "No."

"Would you like to get something to eat with me?" Saber looked hopeful and confident. Tempting. "My treat," Saber added when Landry didn't answer right away.

Landry checked his watch to buy himself some time. This was such a horrible idea. "Okay."

Saber's triumphant smile froze Landry's brain, saving him from regret. "Do you know where Point Grill is?"

Landry nodded. "On Westergard."

"That's where I'm headed, in case we get separated. See you there."

"Okay." Landry watched Saber return to his bike a second time. The show was every bit as sexy. This time, Landry's mind was too busy recovering from the shock of his stupid decisions to let the sight affect him. Landry's dick stirred, proving he didn't need his brain to want Saber. Fuck. That was it. He was calling Nolan the first free minute he had. No way could he keep making decisions under these deprived circumstances. God only knows what stupid thing he'd do next.

TWO

Point Grill was dark and unwelcoming, but they had great burgers. Saber had chosen the place based on the dark part. He enjoyed the thought of an intimate setting. A loud restaurant filled with patrons would hinder his ability to get to know Landry. The poor guy already looked like he questioned his sanity over accepting Saber's invitation. Landry had gotten him hard, if only for a moment. Saber wanted more.

Landry fiddled with his menu and looked around as if searching for the nearest exit.

Saber smirked. The tiger in him relished a chase. His body demanded immediate attention. "Why are you nervous?"

In a show of defiance, Landry's hands fell still.

His gaze met Saber's without wavering. "I'm not nervous."

Saber's smirk grew. "Then are you expecting an attack? I've never seen a man eye the exit so hard."

Landry's gaze moved over Saber's features, searching for something only he knew. "I've never been invited to lunch after issuing a ticket."

"I like to be unpredictable."

Landry's mouth lifted in one corner. He shook his head, as if he still couldn't believe this was happening, but he didn't back down. "What do you do for a living?" Landry asked, obviously determined to infuse some normalcy into their date.

"I'm independently wealthy." It was only partly a lie. "It was a joke," Saber added when Landry looked horrified. "You didn't just accept a date with a drug dealer. I'm a fish and wildlife technician for the state."

Landry laughed. The sound made Saber's stomach quiver. "I didn't think you were a drug dealer."

"Yeah, you kind of did," Saber argued with a laugh. "That's okay, though. We didn't meet under the best of circumstances."

Water appeared in front of them. "What can I get you?"

Saber didn't spare the waitress a glance. His gaze refused to budge from Landry. "Do you know what you want, or do you need more time?"

Hunger lit Landry's stare. His thoughts caressed Saber's brain in the lightest touch. *You*. Saber went hard again, forcing him to fight for air and battle his nature. His gums itched as his teeth tried to lengthen. The animal inside stirred—restless. He'd never heard a human's thoughts before. Sometimes, he caught flashes of other Weres—smaller animals he could dominate, but never a human. Yet, he'd heard Landry. The beast barely contained inside him wanted to take control—claim Landry.

Landry passed his menu to the waitress. "The club sandwich, please?"

Saber handed his menu off as well. "Cheeseburger rare. Thanks."

Landry eyed him, looking nervous, as if he sensed the beast attempting to burst from Saber. "When did you move to the US?"

"Too long ago to recall." That wasn't the least bit true, but Saber could hardly be honest. One hundred and eighty years ago wasn't believable to a human.

"I figured you must've been young, since you don't have an accent."

Saber nodded. "Most people don't realize I'm not

a local. How long have you been a police officer?" Saber needed to turn the conversation away from himself. The more lies he told, the harder they would be to remember. He didn't want to be dishonest with Landry.

Landry sipped his water before answering. "Sixteen years." When Saber's eyebrows rose in surprise, Landry chuckled. "Yes, I'm way too old for you."

That was the most ridiculous thing Saber had ever heard. According to his license, he was twenty-nine. It was only wrong by about two hundred years. "You can spare me that bullshit. Everyone is only as old as they feel."

"Oh great," Landry said, bringing his glass to his mouth. "I only feel like I'm ninety."

Saber couldn't stop smiling. "See. We're closer in age than you thought."

Landry set his glass aside but didn't stop fingering it. His nervousness obviously hadn't abated. "You don't drive like you're ninety."

Without thought, Saber tugged Landry's hand away from his glass and dragged it beneath the table. He toyed with the man's fingers as he held his stare. "There's no reason for you to be so uncomfortable.

You drove here. If you want, you can get up and leave anytime you like." He trailed his finger down the center of Landry's palm, trying to soothe him with his touch and voice. "Tell me about your family."

For a moment, Landry stared at him in silence. He didn't pull away. "My parents live in a retirement community outside of Nashville. I have family up that way they wanted to be closer to. My brother, Shepherd, lives in Flowood. It's not that long of a drive, but we both work and rarely see each other. Otherwise, that's about it."

"You're a workaholic, aren't you?"

Landry smiled. "How did you guess?"

Saber shrugged. "The only reason you'd be this uncomfortable going to lunch is if you either honest to god think I'm a criminal or if you never go out. The only reason someone who looks like you would never go out is if you work all the time because I know you're not hard up for offers."

Landry looked away, but he wasn't quick enough to hide his blush. The hunger rising inside Saber doubled. "I don't get long for lunch."

As if the universe heard him and took mercy, their food arrived. Saber released Landry's hand, even though he didn't want to.

"Do you have any plans tonight?" Saber couldn't let this go with one lunch date.

Landry nodded. "I'm meeting my brother later."

Disappointment slapped him, but Saber didn't let it deter him. "Is your brother older or younger?" Saber took a bite and waited for Landry's answer. If he didn't have long, he needed to let Landry eat, but he also wanted to know everything.

"Older by five years. Growing up, he didn't like me very much since he didn't like sharing our parents and I was annoying. After he moved out, we both tried a little harder."

"I bet you were an adorable kid."

Landry's laugh was a soothing sound. It made Saber want to move closer. "I was a smartass. What about you? Do you have any siblings?"

Saber fought for oxygen for a moment. "I had a twin."

Landry's gaze slid his way again. "I'm sorry."

To hide his hurt, Saber took another bite. Some things were better left unsaid. He swallowed, washing his hurt down with a chunk of burger. "She had an abusive spouse." Which really wasn't uncommon among tigers and was one of the many reasons he stayed far away from his kind. He preferred sticking with the wolf pack if he hung around with anyone. Tigers were mostly solitary.

"Now I'm almost afraid to ask. What about your parents?"

The fact that Landry obviously cared had Saber's smile returning. "They're back living in India. In separate territories. We rarely see each other." It would be hard for a human to understand. His kind didn't have the same family dynamics. Tigers mated for life but didn't necessarily always live together. It was another reason he preferred wolves. Saber hadn't found his mate yet, but he hoped, when he did, they'd stay together. Being together yet apart didn't sound like his version of living. He wanted happiness. Not just existence.

"Same here. It's just not that easy to visit. I feel guilty, but when I finally have a few days off, I don't want to spend it traveling everywhere to visit family. It'll bite me in the ass one day when they're no longer around."

Saber nodded his understanding. He gave Landry a few minutes peace so he could eat. It was important to him that Landry had his needs met. The second the man finished, Saber jumped back in with both feet. "Do you have plans for tomorrow night?"

The smile stretching Landry's lips almost distracted him. "No."

"We should do something."

"What do you have in mind?"

Saber shrugged. "I'm not picky." Plus, he didn't know what humans did for fun. "Let me take you out, and we'll figure out something."

Landry had a way of looking at him that made Saber feel like he stared into his soul. His gaze moved over Saber's features, focusing on Saber's mouth for long enough Saber felt himself leaning forward, falling into the man's eyes. "Sure. Program my number into your phone."

He couldn't remember the last time someone made him so happy with the smallest thing. Saber dug out his phone and programmed Landry's number, grabbing his address too while he was at it. Landry lived in town. That was interesting. Personally, Saber didn't know how he stood the noise.

"I need to get back to work." With one statement, Landry filled Saber with disappointment. He didn't want to let Landry go. Saber couldn't explain it. It didn't seem as if anything special happened between them. There hadn't been any of his usual heavy flirting, over-the-top touching, or extended eye contact—like Saber tended to do. None of that mattered to Saber this time. He just wanted to sit with Landry for no reason at all.

"I'll walk you to your car." Saber motioned to their waitress. When he had her attention, he made sure she watched him drop a fifty on the table. She nodded, and he found himself helping Landry to his feet. When Landry didn't balk, Saber didn't release his hand.

"Thank you for lunch. I feel better about my decision to give you a pass."

Saber nodded. "I get that. No doubt you see the worst of humanity all day. I had an off morning." He flashed Landry a smile. "Even though I can't claim I'm not usually reckless, my bursts of restless energy don't normally endanger other people."

"That's good." Landry looked over. Their gazes met and held. "But I don't want you to get hurt either."

Something inside Saber broke down. He couldn't take another second of being good and not taking charge. As they reached the door, Saber took control and steered Landry inside the bathroom instead before he could get away. Landry looked ready to bolt as Saber locked the door behind them.

"I'm sorry. I can't let you go yet." Saber claimed

the man's mouth before any protest fell from his lips. He couldn't let Landry leave without tasting him. Landry was in uniform and driving his police-issued car. Saber couldn't kiss him outside where the world would see and risk someone complaining about Landry. Plus, Saber planned to stroke every place he could reach. In the middle of the day, outside wasn't a good choice. Not for Saber's sake, but Landry's. Saber wouldn't get the man in trouble with his job.

For a moment, Landry stood completely still beneath Saber's lips—like he'd frozen. Then the man's tongue tentatively touched Saber's bottom lip, as if tasting him. Heat exploded through Saber like an inferno. Landry kissed Saber back, making Saber wonder which of them was in control. His touch was rough. He bit Saber's lip. Saber caught himself holding Landry's ass and rocking against him, intent on fucking him in his clothes. Yeah, he was hard. Once again, Saber considered the spell might've worn off and Landry was the first to touch him afterward. This might be nothing more than months of frustration. That didn't stop Saber from doing his damnedest to come in his jeans.

Saber's mouth moved to Landry's jaw. He nipped before heading for the man's throat. "I won't make you late," he promised even as he sucked at

Landry's skin. Landry's dick was in his hand and Saber didn't know how it happened. He couldn't stop trying to get closer. Without an ounce of hesitation, Saber stroked. "Okay, you might be a few minutes late." He needed Landry's orgasm. It was like he couldn't breathe at the thought of leaving Landry unsatisfied. Saber couldn't explain his desperation. Normally, he only cared about his partner's pleasure when it led to his. This was different. As horny and deprived as Saber was, nothing mattered except Landry. Landry's lust was pressing on his chest and brain, suffocating him while making him stupid. Saber pumped at Landry's cock, treating the man's pleasure as if it was his own. He needed Landry to come. Saber didn't know what would happen when he did, but Saber knew something would. He reclaimed Landry's mouth, kissing him deep. Landry tore at his skin, trying to get closer as desperate-sounding moans vibrated through their kiss. He felt Landry tense. Saber quickly covered Landry's dick with his t-shirt, keeping the man's cum from hitting his dark uniform. The sound Landry made as he blew almost stole Saber's orgasm without a single touch to his cock. The inside of Saber's underwear was uncomfortably wet, and his stomach was coated in Landry's cum. It didn't matter. He'd made Landry fly. The tiger inside him roared with satisfaction.

Harsh breaths filled the tiny restroom. Landry held Saber's shoulders in a tight grip. "What the fuck just happened?"

Saber brushed his lips across Landry's neck. "You just ruined my shirt."

A low chuckle vibrated from Landry's throat. "I'll buy you a new one."

"The fuck you say. I hope you ruin several more." Saber stole another kiss before Landry came down from his high and realized what he'd done. "I need to get cleaned up. You should leave out of here first so you're not too late getting back to work." Saber fixed Landry's clothes as he made the suggestion.

Landry held his stare for a moment before giving him a sharp nod. He started toward the door. Saber stopped him. "Thank you for taking a chance on me. Tomorrow night, I'll try harder to behave."

A bright smile lit Landry's face. This time, he was the one who kissed Saber. It was quick, but Saber's heart skipped a beat. "See you tomorrow." Without looking back, he slipped from the bathroom. Saber stared into space, trying to figure out what the fuck was happening to his life. His chest still felt funny, and he wasn't the least bit turned on. It was like Landry had taken Saber's life source with him when he left. Saber was still happy and excited about seeing Landry again. But the raging lust that had him leaking in his jeans while holding Landry was completely gone. Saber had thought to finish himself off once he was alone, but nope. His body was once again his enemy. Fuck. He'd never been more confused.

THREE

Cars and motorcycles filled the parking lot of Raff's Pool Hall. Even though Landry didn't see Shepherd's truck, he still headed for the door. If his brother wasn't there yet, Landry would grab a beer and try to commandeer an empty table. The sound of billiard balls cracking against one another filled the air inside the bar as well as laughter and voices. Landry's gaze swept the room, searching for Shepherd. He spotted Saber first and his brother second. It was like a shot to the gut. Saber looked every bit as sexy as he had earlier in the day. This time, he wore a black t-shirt and well-worn jeans. Each item still strained against Saber's muscles. That wasn't why Landry couldn't breathe. A bright, devilish smile stretched Saber's lips as he felt up a woman, practically grinding against her ass as he "helped" her line up a shot. As Landry looked on, Saber's nose went into the air, as if he caught a familiar scent. His gaze landed on Landry with laser-like focus—like he'd spotted his prey. Landry's gaze moved from Saber's unnaturally light blue eyes to the blonde woman Saber had pinned against the pool table. He'd known from the first time he set eyes on Saber the man was a player. That didn't make the sight any less bruising to his pride. Landry turned away and headed for his brother's table, leaving no room for doubt he'd dismissed Saber. Saber might be used to having whoever he wanted whenever he wanted, but Landry didn't play that game. He didn't enjoy the thought of being just another stop in a long line of lovers.

As he headed Shepherd's way, his brother's face lit. They were complete opposites. Anyone who met them and not their parents would think they weren't related. Landry looked exactly like his mom, except for his eyes. Those were his dad's. Shepherd looked exactly like their dad—blond and wide-shouldered. Except for Shepherd's eyes; those he got from their mom. No one could claim they were the mailman's babies, but they didn't look like brothers.

Shepherd came to his feet and pulled Landry

into a one-armed hug. "Baby brother." He said the words so loud Landry didn't doubt everyone heard him a town over. It was beyond obvious he'd been drinking a while.

"Shep. How's it going, old man?"

"Amazing. I got a promotion today. That's why I had to come celebrate with my favorite people."

"That's fantastic." Landry infused as much as happiness as he could in the words. His brother deserved the world. Life hadn't been easy for him the past few years. He'd joined the Marines and gotten married right out of high school. After being deployed more than he was home, his wife left him for some little guy who owned a flower shop. It had been a huge blow to Shepherd's pride and shattered his heart. Personally, Landry had always hated Shauna and was glad to see her go, but his heart broke for his brother. There was no one nicer on the planet.

Landry's gaze moved to the second man at the table. Frankie Moore had been Shepherd's best friend since the eighth grade and might as well be family. Personally, Landry hated him too, but Shepherd always had bad taste in people. Still, Landry tried his best to be nice. "Hey, Frankie.

How's it going?" Landry pulled out a chair at the table and sat.

The red-haired man focused on Landry, looking more drunk than Shepherd. "I'm drunk. You gonna arrest me?" He punctuated the question with a loud and obnoxious laugh.

Landry held on to his smile, even as he winced at the sound. "I'm off duty." He switched his attention to Shepherd. "Just don't drive home, okay?"

Shepherd waved off his concern. "Don't worry. I'm staying at the motel down the road so I don't have to make the two-hour drive home. I'll just walk, and Frankie's old lady is picking him up later."

Frankie snorted into his beer. "The bitch is still good for a few things."

Landry fought the urge to rub the spot between his eyes where a pain bloomed. He loved his brother, Landry reminded himself. Otherwise, there was no way he could tolerate Frankie. Frankie had also married his high-school sweetheart right out of school. In his case, he didn't deserve such a nice woman. If Landry could've picked anyone for Shepherd, it would be Frankie's wife, Tabitha. She was blonde-haired and green-eyed just like Shepherd. They would make a beautiful couple. Shepherd sure as fuck would treat her better.

"How is Tabitha these days?" Landry asked, trying to be civil.

Frankie's dark-brown gaze moved over Landry's features, as if looking for something behind Landry's inquiry. "What do you care? I thought you liked men."

Landry lost the battle not to rub his forehead.

Shepherd slapped Frankie on the shoulder and squeezed. "Don't start shit tonight, man. We're celebrating." Even though Shepherd's voice stayed jovial, Frankie winced at the pressure on his shoulder. Landry bit the inside of his cheek to keep from laughing. Even though he didn't need him to be, Shepherd was still the overprotective older brother. The guy was like a fucking bull—stronger and bigger than he realized. Years of staying in fighting shape coupled with several more years of working in a steel mill had turned his brother into a mountain. Shepherd dropped his hand to the table. "Tell us about your life. What's new in the world of Landry?"

Landry shrugged. "Not a thing, really. Still just working and not much else."

Shepherd shook his head. His eyes lost some of their happiness. "You need more than that, baby brother. I know you take your job seriously and all that, but there's more to life. You need a nice guy. Whatever happened to Nolan?"

"Nolan is just a friend." The kind of friend that let Landry fuck him on occasion but still only a friend. Landry didn't feel the need to add that tidbit. Instead, he turned the conversation Shepherd's way. "What about you? Surely you have someone chasing you. You always do." It was true. Women loved Shepherd. He was just too damn nice to notice.

Happiness lit Shepherd's eyes once more. "Nah. I..." Shepherd's gaze moved to a spot over Landry's shoulder. The hair rose on the back of Landry's neck.

"Officer LaTour, we meet again. Can I buy you a drink?"

Goosebumps rose on Landry's skin as the too cocky voice caressed his ears. Landry fought to keep his face smooth and his tone cool. He didn't look Saber's way. "Mr. Khatri. The world is very small. I think I'll pass."

Shepherd's gaze moved between them, as if trying to figure out what he was witnessing.

Saber didn't give up. He snagged a chair from a nearby table and sat. His warm breath fanned across Landry's neck as Saber draped his arm across the back of Landry's chair and leaned close to his ear.

"If I didn't know better, I'd say you were stalking me. Since I know that's not the case, it must be fate."

Possibly Saber came here all the time. Landry wouldn't know. He never came here unless his brother wanted to meet. Landry turned his head and focused on Saber. Up close, all Landry could think about was their kiss. Saber's sexy full lips had been on Landry's body. No doubt they'd already been on five people since then. "I'm here with my brother." Landry hoped Saber would take a hint.

Instead, Saber focused on Shepherd, as if he knew exactly which man at the table was Landry's brother. He reached across the table and held his hand out for Shepherd. "I'm Landry's friend Saber. You must be Shepherd. I've heard a lot about you."

Shepherd brightened as he shook Saber's hand. "It's very nice to meet you. I never get to meet any of Landry's friends anymore. Not since I moved to Flowood."

Saber motioned toward Shepherd's and Frankie's drinks. "It looks like you're celebrating."

Frankie nodded. "Shep got promoted to floor supervisor at the steel mill today."

Landry couldn't stop staring at Saber. He looked genuinely impressed and happy for Shepherd, even though they'd never met before now. "That's great news. Let me buy the three of you a round."

Landry opened his mouth to protest. Shepherd cut him off. "Thanks, man. That's awesome."

Saber motioned toward the bar. Landry wondered how he expected the bartender to know what he wanted. Before he had time to mull it over, a waitress arrived with four beers. Not only were they exactly what Frankie and Shepherd had been drinking, the woman handed Landry a light beer—like he would've ordered. Saber didn't look his way, but neither did he move his arm from the back of Saber's chair.

"So how do you know my baby brother?" Shepherd asked, keeping Saber there.

A sexy rumble of laughter came from Saber's chest. Landry's body stirred at the sound. "He pulled me over for speeding and gave me a ticket. I took him to lunch."

Frankie snorted. It was an ugly sound. "He gave you a ticket, and you bought him lunch? You should've told him to go fuck himself. Landry has always been too pious."

Landry took a breath and counted to twenty. He was here for his brother. The lightest of touches brushed Landry's shoulder as if Saber couldn't resist caressing him. Against his will, Landry's gaze slid Saber's way. He was smiling. The gesture screamed overconfidence, but Saber's eyes were like ice as they locked on Frankie.

"I also gave him a hand job in the bathroom, so maybe not as pious as you think, and definitely worth it."

Torn between horror and humor, Landry stared at his drink, unblinking.

Frankie didn't take the hint and back down. "You don't look like a queer."

The entire bar went silent. A shadow fell over the table, bringing Landry's head up. The overly muscular man who worked the bar stood over them. His eyes were an odd shade of amber and he was graying at the temples. A week's worth of growth covered his hard jaw. His gaze looked cold and deadly while locked on Frankie. Saber's fingertips lightly stroked the back of Landry's arm—up and down. Soothing.

When the huge dude spoke, his tone was twice as cold as his stare. "Watch your words if you want to stay."

Frankie blinked, as if trying to decide how to react. "I meant no offense."

The way the man's amber-colored eyes didn't

waver gave Landry the impression he knew it was a lie. "Even if Saber hadn't just bought you a drink, your words still would've been rude. Considering it looks like you're enjoying that beer, your actions are twice as offensive. That shit doesn't fly under my roof."

Frankie's gaze moved to Saber. "Sorry. Like I said, I didn't mean anything by it."

The amber gaze moved Shepherd's way. "Did I hear you say you worked at the mill in Flowood?"

Landry sifted through their conversation. He was absolutely certain no one had mentioned the exact location of Shepherd's job. Still, Shepherd smiled. "Yes. I'm the daytime floor supervisor over there."

The guy circled the table and pulled up a chair next to Shepherd. "I have a cousin who works there."

Shepherd was all in. If he cared about Frankie nearly losing his life, Shepherd didn't show it. His overly friendly nature was in full view. He focused on the new addition at the table and smiled like he couldn't wait to know more. "Really? Who's your cousin?"

"Wesley Yates."

A loud laugh escaped Shepherd, making Landry smile at the sound. "Yep. I know Wesley.

He's been a crane operator over there as long as I've been there. We eat lunch together every day. I'm Shepherd." He held his hand out to the stranger.

The man accepted his handshake. "Raff."

"Oh, you were serious. This is actually your roof."

Raff's face softened, making him look human as humor flashed in his eyes. "Yeah. I inherited the place from my dad."

Before Shepherd could respond, another man appeared at the edge of the table. He grabbed a chair and squeezed between Frankie and Shepherd, joining the conversation like he'd been there the whole time. "So you see Wesley every day. I'm sorry for that." Landry couldn't look away from the show. The new arrival had long dark hair that flowed down his back and his eyes were an odd shade Landry couldn't make out because they caught the light, seeming to glow.

Frankie found his tongue. He laughed. "Dude, pirates went out of style two years ago."

Landry's eyebrows rose. As rude as Frankie's remark was, Landry damn near snapped his fingers in an ah-ha moment. The guy did remind him of a pirate. He couldn't place why. It was not like he was dressed like one. There was just something about him.

The guy's strange gaze moved Frankie's way. His voice took on an enticing edge. "Your wife is on the way. After you apologize to everyone for being such a dick, you should go wait for her in the parking lot. When she gets here, you need to lavish her with praise for ever marrying the likes of you." He looked away and focused on Shepherd. "I'm Dante."

As they shook hands, Frankie moved to his feet. "Hey, guys, I'm sorry for being a dick tonight. Too much alcohol, I guess. Tabitha is on her way. I'd better wait on her outside so she doesn't have to brave this rough crowd." Without waiting for anyone to respond, Frankie walked away.

Landry stared at the spot where he'd been, trying to decide what the fuck he'd just witnessed. Before he could think of a single thing to say, Raff's conversation with Shepherd cut through his thoughts.

"If you hang out with us until closing, we'll give you a ride to the motel. This is a dangerous place to be late at night. You shouldn't walk. There are wild animals that hunt at night around here."

Saber's warm lips brushed the shell of his ear, stealing Landry from the conversation happening across from him. His body stirred as Saber's breath caressed him. "Where would you like to go tomorrow night?"

Landry turned his head. Saber was too close. All he had to do was lean in an inch and their lips would touch. The temptation was winning. He hardened his heart against it. "You seem a little too busy for me. I'm not much on being just another number you keep stashed away for a rainy day."

To his surprise, Saber didn't look a bit contrite. He smirked. "Everyone here knows I'm a flirt. They also know they shouldn't take it seriously. I always go home alone."

A snort escaped Landry before he could call it back. "Going home alone means nothing other than you care about no one. You don't need a bed to fuck everything that moves." Landry had never been the jealous type. He'd always believed jealousy was an ugly thing on everyone equally. Landry still believed that. Yet here he was—incapable of not snapping at Saber like a petty teenager. He shouldn't care. It wasn't his business if Saber fucked everyone he met. They weren't a couple. Landry couldn't explain why seeing Saber's body molded against someone else as he'd come through the door had gutted him. But it had, and Landry didn't want more. Being with Saber would always be that way. Landry felt it in his gut.

Saber's fingers stroked the back of Landry's arm again. "Let's go outside. Give me ten more minutes of your time."

A resounding "no" rose in Landry's throat. Something sad passed over Saber's features, as if he knew what Landry would say. The idea of hurting Saber hit Landry harder than the sight of Saber pressed against someone else. "Ten minutes," he said, pushing to his feet. He already regretted his decision, but that didn't stop him. Landry focused on his brother. "We'll be back in a few. Are you good?"

Shepherd flashed him a smile. "Sure." He went back to staring at Raff before the word fully died on his lips. Landry stared a moment longer. There was something odd happening with Shepherd and the pair flanking him. If Landry didn't know better... Saber's hand slid across the small of Landry's back, cutting off his line of thinking. He headed for the door with Saber at his side, hoping against hope he wasn't as big of a fool as he suspected. Landry would find out soon enough.

THE NOISE of the crowd died away as the door closed behind them. Saber couldn't take his eyes off Landry. From the moment he'd caught Landry's scent in the air, he'd been hooked. Landry looked sexy as hell. Saber had thought it wasn't possible for the man to be hotter than he was in uniform. Until he walked through the door tonight and proved Saber wrong. In jeans that cupped the man's every asset and a t-shirt that molded against his cut chest, Landry swelled Saber's tongue with desire. Saber had brushed aside the woman he'd been flirting with for half an hour and been at Landry's side in an instant. There was no one else who compared to him.

Landry eyed the guy who'd been sitting with them as they passed him in the parking lot. He stared at the road, unblinking and waiting for a wife that was probably still hours away from arrival. Saber bit back a laugh. Normally, he wasn't one to find a vampire's mind control funny, but Frankie was a douche. He'd had it coming with his rudeness. Saber owed Raff and Dante a drink for distracting Shepherd. Otherwise, Landry wouldn't have agreed to leave his brother alone for ten minutes. Saber could feel the man's loyalty each time he glanced his brother's way. They were obviously close. Saber swallowed his jealousy. He had no one and sometimes the knowledge slapped him at the oddest times. It was good Landry wasn't alone in the world. Saber caressed the small of Landry's back as he slipped his arm around Landry's waist. He would never want Landry to endure hundreds of years alone as Saber had. The thought alone had Saber's chest aching. He led Landry to his bike and handed Landry his helmet.

Landry eyed it. "You said we were going outside. I didn't agree to leave."

With a sigh, Saber closed the space between them and put the helmet on Landry's head. He buckled it before Landry could get away. "Quit being difficult. I don't think you're some piece of ass I'll never think of again or that you're an idiot I can jerk around. This isn't about any of that."

For a moment, Landry blinked, as if trying to decide how Saber read his mind and repeated his thoughts. "You don't have a helmet now. It's the law."

Laughter tumbled out without Saber's permission. "Stop being a cop for a few minutes. I'm not that easy to kill and we're not going that far." He straddled the bike and waited, half expecting Landry to refuse. With a loud, exasperated sigh, Landry climbed on behind him. Saber's eyes fell closed as

Landry's body molded against his. He savored the sensation of Landry's arms encircling him. His fingers lightly caressed Saber's stomach. The breath left his lungs. He needed to have Landry to himself. Saber fired the bike to life and eased away. As he hit the back roads, his speed increased. The faster he went, the closer Landry got. He almost sped past his driveway because he didn't want the moment to end, but Landry wouldn't want to stay gone all night.

As he pulled in next to his cabin, Saber glanced over his shoulder. "Can you remember how to get here?"

"Yes," Landry said as he climbed from the bike and removed the helmet.

Saber gave him a sharp nod. "Good. This is my place. In case you ever need me."

Landry looked around. "How much land do you have out here?"

Saber tried seeing the place through a visitor's eyes. His cabin was on the small side, but it was big enough for him. It was built on the edge of the lake. To him, the place was beautiful, peaceful, and private. It gave him freedom to roam, run, and hunt. To Landry, it was probably none of those things. "Eighty acres. My closest neighbor is Raff."

With the helmet hugged to his chest, Landry

turned in a slow circle before looking up at the sky. The stars were bright. "It's peaceful here." He dropped his gaze to Saber's. "And beautiful."

Saber nodded. The lump in his throat wouldn't let him do more.

When Saber didn't say anything, Landry shifted nervously. "So, Raff is your neighbor. It seems like everyone knows everyone around here."

Latching on to the subject, Saber forced his tongue to work. "Yeah. It's a small parish. Strangers don't come around often. I guess that's why I was so surprised to see you tonight."

Landry flashed him a smile. "Judging by the way I found you, I imagine so." Before Saber could defend himself, Landry moved on. "My brother goes to the pool hall when he's in town, which isn't often. I've been with him a time or two in the past. It's not really my scene. Plus, it's a bit out of the way for me." A line appeared between Landry's eyes. "What made you bring me here? It's obvious you're not interested in anything serious."

Saber closed the distance between them. "You should really get to know me better before continuing with the assumptions. I almost embarrassed you earlier today. That wasn't my intent. This time, I wanted to take you where there was no chance of harming your reputation when I kiss you."

Landry flattened his palm against Saber's chest, stopping him from getting close enough to do as he claimed. "I'm not sure if that's true."

Saber felt his face screw up in confusion. "What?"

"I don't think you're worried over my reputation. In fact, I'm almost certain you're more concerned what people think of you if you're seen kissing me, or maybe you're just a player who wants to ensure he can move on to the next victim when I leave tonight. Either way, I get the impression you're never serious. The thing is, I'm always serious. Probably that makes me boring, but the only thing I have is my sixteen-year-long career, and you strike me as the type to leave people's lives in shambles while you skip away. I'm not trying to insult you."

Saber wasn't sure that was true. There was a tiny part of Saber that thought he probably should be insulted. The rest of him understood. There was something between them. Even with only human instinct to rely on, Saber knew Landry felt it too. Landry was right to be scared. "I know you don't have any reason to trust me, but I'm not out to hurt you."

The spot where Landry held him away turned into more of a caress. "I'm not saying I don't want you to kiss me." The words came out soft and sexy. "I'm also not saying I don't want to see you again."

Saber couldn't stop staring at Landry's lips, but the man wasn't letting him any closer. "What are you saying?"

"That you should think about what you want," Landry answered, bringing Saber's gaze back to Landry's gorgeous eyes. "If you decide chances are good I'll be catching you with someone else every time I turn around or scraping you off the road when you can't behave, then stay away. I won't hold it against you if you don't show tomorrow night."

If Landry was anyone else, Saber would give his speech about how he was free to do as pleased. No one ever took him seriously because he was never serious. Saber wasn't sure that was true with Landry. Maybe he really did need to think this through. "Okay."

Landry caressed Saber's chest again. His hand fell away, and he shook his head. "I'm sorry. You don't owe me anything." He scrubbed at his forehead. "To be honest, I don't really know what happened earlier. When I came through the door... I don't know. Just never mind." He rubbed his forehead again. "In your shoes, I wouldn't show up tomorrow night. I just..." Landry looked crestfallen and confused.

In a lightning quick move, Saber snagged the back of Landry's neck and hauled him forward. Their lips met. Landry came at him every bit as wild. "There's something about you," Saber said between kisses. The helmet fell to the ground. Landry buried his fingers in Saber's hair and pulled him even closer. Every time Landry touched him, Saber forgot about his own needs. All he cared about was making Landry happy. Another first. He knew Landry was confused. Saber probably set off every warning bell in the man's head. Whatever it took, Saber wouldn't hurt him.

Saber pulled away enough to meet Landry's stare. He massaged Landry's hips, needing to keep touching him. "Your cum is still all over my t-shirt. I couldn't put it in the wash."

A smile lit Landry's eyes. "Why?"

"Because it's covered in your cum," Saber explained, feeling it was enough. He bent and snagged the helmet from the ground. Without thought, his lips brushed Landry's stomach on the way back up. His eyes fell closed as Landry sucked in a hiss at the contact. If he ever had a night where they were alone with nothing but time, Saber would ruin Landry for anyone else. "I promised ten minutes." He put the helmet back on Landry. As he buckled it, Saber stole another kiss. He was getting addicted. "Damn, you're beautiful. I need to get you back before I break my word and keep you."

Landry smiled and shook his head as if he didn't know what to do with Saber. Saber hoped he chose to keep him. The ride back moved slower. Saber couldn't force himself to pick up speed. He was in no hurry to return Landry to his brother. No matter how slow he moved, there was no putting off the inevitable. Saber snagged the same parking spot. As Landry climbed from the back and removed his helmet, he stared toward the door. Saber followed his gaze and found Frankie standing in the same spot as he'd been when they left.

"Why is he acting like that?"

Saber shrugged. "People act stupid when they're drinking. I get the feeling that guy is an idiot even when he's sober."

Even with Saber's half-assed explanation, Landry headed Frankie's way. "Hey, man. I don't think Tabitha is coming quite yet."

Frankie's gaze never wavered from the road. "Nope. She's coming."

Landry didn't give up. "Why don't you wait on her inside? Tabitha is a tough girl. She can rough the crowd to find you when she gets here."

Frankie shook his head. "I have to wait here. I have too much to say to her."

For a moment, Landry stared at Frankie in obvious confusion. "Whatever," he finally said, heading for the door. Saber rushed ahead of him and held the door open. Landry glanced his way and winked as he passed. The gesture did something odd to Saber's chest. He couldn't wait for tomorrow night.

Even though he realized his time was up, Saber still followed Landry to the corner where he'd left Shepherd. The table was filled with different people and Shepherd was nowhere to be seen. Landry looked to Saber as if he had the answer. On the sly, Saber sniffed the air. There wasn't a hint of Shepherd any longer. Saber's gaze moved toward the bar. Raff wasn't there. In his place was a red-haired woman who occasionally worked on Raff's nights off. He headed her way.

"Hey, Ashka. Where did Raff run off to?"

Her gold gaze moved his way. It was her duty to protect Raff as the alpha of her pack, but she'd always shown a soft spot for Saber. He used it to his advantage now. She eyed him with obvious interest. "Dante and he went home for the night."

"Do you know if he had a..." Saber glanced Landry's way, catching himself before calling Shepherd a human. "... blond guy with him? Big guy. Lots of muscle."

Ashka's gaze move Landry's way before returning to Saber. "Yeah. He took Shepherd with him."

He winked. "Thanks, doll." When he focused on Landry once more, Landry had a deep line between his brows. Saber couldn't decide if he was pissed off over Saber flirting or confused as fuck.

When Landry noticed Saber watching him, his face cleared. "Looks like Shepherd made a lot of friends while we were gone."

Saber leaned against the edge of the bar. "He seems like a friendly guy."

Landry's mouth lifted in one corner. "Well, since I lost my brother, I guess I'll head home."

"Or," Saber said, closing the distance between them and herding him toward the door. "You could admit you're free now and spend some more time with me."

"I have to work tomorrow."

Saber smelled victory. "I won't keep you out late."

Landry's chest expanded on a deep breath. "What did you have in mind?"

After slinging his arm over Landry's shoulders, Saber headed for the parking lot. "Where's your car?"

As they passed Frankie, Landry shook his head and pointed toward a black SUV with tinted windows parked in the darkest corner of the lot. "Right there."

"Awesome," Saber breathed, never meaning anything more. "Let's go steam up the windows."

A loud laugh escaped Landry, making Saber smile at the sound. "What the hell. It can't be worse than a public restroom."

"My thoughts exactly," Saber said with a smile that felt evil even to him. He couldn't wait to do nothing other than kiss Landry for the next couple of hours. It sounded like a night in heaven to him.

FOUR

Landry couldn't stop smiling. He couldn't remember the last time he'd made out like a freaking teenager in his car. There was a damn hickey on his chest. A hickey. He shook his head every time he thought it. Landry felt twenty years younger. Even waking up at four in the morning to hit the gym hadn't bothered him. Normally, he dragged himself from bed with nothing to look forward to. Now he was minutes away from seeing Saber again and Landry was afraid if he looked in the mirror, he'd see that he glowed. Saber hadn't told him what to wear or what they were doing. He'd gone with a maroon t-shirt and dark jeans, hoping the outfit would work for whatever. By the time a knock landed on his door,

Landry was already pacing the floor. He had no idea why he was so nervous.

Landry opened the door to the hottest sight he'd ever seen. Saber's long hair was pulled back away from his face. The man's tank top showed off huge, cut arms. Against his will, Landry's gaze dropped to the toes of Saber's worn-looking work boots. His long legs were encased in well-worn jeans that hugged his massive thighs. Landry's mouth watered. When he met Saber's stare, Saber didn't look offended by Landry's blatant inspection. In fact, Landry got the impression he was waiting to have Landry's attention.

"You look amazing. Good enough to eat."

Landry snorted out a laugh at the compliment. Saber growled the words—like an animal. It was damn sexy. "So do you."

"How do you feel about fishing?"

Saber's question caught Landry off guard. "I have done it once or twice."

Saber clasped his hands in front of him and dropped his chin like he was giving Landry his whole attention or teaching a class. "Okay. How do you feel about night fishing?"

Landry's eyebrows rose. "With like the alligators and whatnot?"

Saber's smile popped into place, giving Landry the impression he was amused. "Yes, with the alligators and stuff."

Landry blinked. He wasn't sure how to react.

Saber's smile grew. "We'll be in a boat. I'll keep you safe. Don't forget this is what I do for a living. I'm a professional." Saber shifted closer, making Landry realize he'd never invited the man inside. Now his tongue wouldn't work. He couldn't stop staring at the cocky tilt to Saber's mouth. "Not to mention, we'll be completely alone. Not another soul around for miles. Under the stars."

"Yes. Let's go." Landry didn't mean to sound quite so enthusiastic, but it was too late to take it back.

"In a minute," Saber said, shuffling even closer. Landry's shirt stretched across his back as Saber hauled him forward. Saber didn't close his eyes as he leaned in. He held Landry's gaze until the last second. Saber's intensity stole Landry's breath. As their lips met, Landry filled with completion. It was ridiculous. They'd just met. But Landry couldn't deny the truth. Saber made him feel like no one else ever had. His chest swelled with an unnamed emotion as their tongues brushed.

Saber pulled back a hair and brushed noses with

Landry, doubling the falling sensation overcoming Landry. "Are you ready to go?"

Landry nodded, but his feet wouldn't budge. His fingers curled around Saber's shirt. For a moment, he considered yanking the man inside and dragging him to bed. His fingers unclenched. He had to behave. "Sure." As he made the claim, Landry locked the door and pulled it closed behind him. "Would you like me to do drive?"

"Nope," Saber said, slinging his arm over Landry's shoulders and steering him toward a silver Camaro. "I want you at my mercy." He opened the passenger side door for Landry.

Landry eyed the car. It was badass. "Is this a sixty-seven?"

"Damn. It's like you were made for me," Saber said with a shake of his head as he closed the door behind Landry. Landry assumed that meant he was right.

They made the drive to Saber's cabin in companionable silence. A few times, Landry wondered if he should try to make conversation, but the way Saber toyed with his fingers as he drove kept Landry's mind too busy to concentrate on anything else. Saber's boat turned out to be a lot bigger than Landry expected. If he'd thought about it, Saber probably spent a lot of time out on the water for work, which—most likely—meant a large boat. Still, Landry was constantly impressed with Saber. The way his muscles tensed and rolled with every move he made kept Landry fascinated.

Landry wasn't much of a fisherman. In truth, without Saber there, he probably would've hated every minute. But the later the night got, and the closer Saber sat, the more Landry enjoyed himself.

Saber maneuvered the boat into a secluded alcove and dropped anchor. "This is my favorite spot," Saber admitted as he pulled Landry to his feet. He settled onto the floor and pulled Landry down to sit between his knees. Once they were settled, Saber wrapped a blanket around them and snuggled close. "Sometimes, I come out here alone and sit all night."

This place suited Saber. It was wild and quiet. Landry looked up, taking in the bright stars. The place was also beautiful—just like Saber. "It seems like you enjoy being alone."

Saber didn't respond right away. Instead, he hugged Landry tighter and kissed his shoulder. Finally, he spoke against Landry's skin. "I don't know that I like to be alone as much as I don't like unnecessary noise or busyness. Most people like to always be doing something, even if it's just watching

TV. As much as I love coming here to be alone and get away from the noise, so far I have to say it's a hundred times better with you."

Landry bit his lip, trying to hide his smile. "Usually, I'm guilty of needing noise to distract me, even though I spend quite a bit of my day alone. It's funny, though. When I'm with you, I don't feel like I have to say anything."

Hot breath blew across his ear as Saber nipped at his earlobe. "I've noticed you're not very talkative," Saber said as he trailed tiny bites down the side of Landry's neck. Chill bumps rose on his skin and his dick hardened. Even though Landry was massively turned on, he didn't feel the need to act on his desires. Instead, he felt lazy—like he wanted nothing more than to soak up Saber's attention. Plus, Saber's actions didn't feel sexual. They felt loving, and that was so much better. It was the one thing Landry had been starved of for a long time. He could call Nolan for sex anytime. There was no one Landry could call for intimacy. "Do you want to hear something funny?"

"Mhmm." It was all the response Landry could muster under the circumstances.

Saber's hand slid across Landry's chest, as if he couldn't stop touching him. "Last night and tonight have been two of the best nights of my life, and I don't even know why. It's just you, I guess. You probably think I'm being corny."

A soft chuckle escaped Landry. "If you are, I'm loving it. I'm also kind of hoping you won't stop."

"I'm not very exciting." Saber said the words quietly, as if confessing a dark secret. "You'll probably get bored with me pretty fast. Most people think I'm fun for one night. After that, they're ready to go party, or whatever h—people do."

Landry wondered what Saber had been about to say before catching himself. "This is one time it'll probably be the other way around for you. I have to get up really early every day and never have the same days off each week. I'm in bed by ten most nights."

Saber lit up his watch and checked the time. It was almost midnight. "Why didn't you say anything? I don't want you in some dangerous situation and too tired to deal with it."

The words caused an odd sensation in Landry's chest. He couldn't remember the last time anyone had cared about anything that had to do with him. "It's fine. I'm off tomorrow."

He felt Saber relax. "Is that so?" Damn. The sultry side of Saber was back.

Landry nodded. "There's no need to hurry."

Saber's arms tightened around him once more. His lips skimmed the cords of Landry's neck. "Mhmm, I have you all to myself for a few hours. I don't even know where to start, but I'm sure I'll think of something." Landry didn't know what Saber had in mind, but he was game for whatever. Maybe Saber would get tired of him before long. Maybe he wouldn't. Either way, Landry intended to enjoy every kiss and touch until that moment came. He wanted everything Saber had to offer.

THE SKY WAS an eerie orange and green, signaling the break of dawn as Saber pulled into Landry's driveway. Saber fought the urge to shake his head. In a lot of ways, they couldn't be less alike. Landry's house looked like every other house in the subdivision where he lived. White siding. Black shutters. Cookie-cutter life. All the lawns were perfectly manicured. It was obvious Landry worshipped order and swam with the crowd. Saber was a loner who lived out in the rough and loved wild freedom. Yet Saber had more fun with Landry, doing nothing but sitting out on the water, than he'd had in years. He didn't want to say goodbye.

"I had a great time."

Saber glanced over at Landry's claim. He looked tired and wind-blown. Sexy. "Me too. I'll walk you to the door."

Landry nodded and slipped from the car. As they met in front, their fingers automatically linked, as if drawn together. Hand in hand, they walked up the steps and onto the porch. The instant Saber had Landry crowded against the door, his mouth found Landry's. Their lips brushed, and then their tongues touched. Saber licked, doing his damnedest to curl his tongue around Landry's. An unnamed emotion grew in his chest with every passing second. He wanted Landry, but it wasn't sexual. Not completely. It was more. Bigger. He wanted to keep him.

"I don't want to leave."

Landry nodded. "You should come in."

Saber's lips wouldn't leave any place he could reach as Landry unlocked the door. He kissed the man's neck, shoulder, and every other place he could as Landry led him through the living room. He saw nothing but Landry. The place could've been filled with people and Saber wouldn't have noticed. The moment they were inside Landry's bedroom, Saber knew it without looking around. He could smell Landry on the air. This was where Landry slept. His scent permeated every surface. Saber tugged at Landry's clothes and did his best to overwhelm him. He touched, kissed, and broke down Landry's walls. It was a siege. Saber was a dominant beast. A predator. Strength also made him a protector and provider. It was his job to make sure Landry's needs were met before his own.

Saber lost his shirt but kept his pants on, even after he'd stripped every stitch from Landry. He couldn't stop kissing and licking, tasting Landry. Saber only caught glimpses of Landry's nude body as his lips moved from one spot to the next. It wasn't until he urged Landry onto the bed that Saber got his first full picture of Landry—unclothed and aroused. For a moment, all Saber could do was stare. Landry was sleek. It was obvious he needed to be in shape for his profession. He wasn't bulky muscle. Landry was tight and solid. Saber needed to touch him.

After setting one knee on the mattress, Saber hooked his arm beneath Landry's knee and drew it upward. He pressed his lips to the soft skin inside Landry's knee before skimming kisses up the man's inner thigh. Landry gasped. Saber's gaze moved to his. Landry's face was flushed. His lips were swollen. He stared down at Saber with hooded eyes. Saber couldn't look away as he moved higher. Landry's cock jumped and leaked onto his stomach. The sight made Saber feel powerful. The need to taste Landry grew inside him, becoming a fevered pitch. He couldn't wait. Saber flattened his tongue against Landry's cock and licked to the man's crown. A sound came from deep inside Landry's chest. Saber wanted more. He lapped at Landry's dick. The more Landry squirmed beneath him and whimpered, the harder Saber tried for more. The inside of Saber's underwear was a swamp of pre-cum. His hips rolled, openly humping the mattress as he pleasured Landry. He could feel himself changing, becoming more animalistic by the second. His tongue thinned, and taste buds changed, becoming prickly, and giving him better control to tug at Landry's cock. Landry writhed, obviously half crazed. Pride filled Saber's chest. His man's pleasure was all that mattered. He ground his erection against the mattress, openly fucking the bed now as he sucked off Landry. Saber sank his claws into the sheets, seeking purchase as Landry's desperation pushed its way inside Saber's mind. They were connected in a way Saber had never experienced before. He didn't know if it was because Landry was human, and his defenses weren't as strong as an immortal.

In that moment, the reasons didn't matter. Saber

could feel Landry's orgasm building. The more the pressure built, the harder Saber worked. He let Landry fuck his mouth, choking him. The sound of Landry's sheets ripping rent the air. They didn't slow. Saber rotated his hips, massaging his erection on the bed. He licked and sucked as vibrations came from his throat. Every sound he made became more animal-like by the second. His gums itched. He fought the impulse to bite—hold Landry in place while he took his pleasure. Satisfying Landry mattered more. Landry's short fingernails scored Saber's skin. The spring inside him wound tighter. An explosion of color slammed into him. Cum flooded his mouth and his underwear. It rolled down his chin and soaked Landry's stomach. Harsh breaths shot through the room. Saber turned his head and his gaze landed on his reflection in a mirror hanging from the open closet door. His eyes were iridescent, his features harder than a human's. Saber's gaze shot to his hands. They were more paw than human. His claws were buried in the covers. Horror raced through him. He was half a breath from transforming.

Saber leapt from the bed. His feet silently hit the floor, further driving his panic. He was in tiger mode.

Saber wasn't sure he could control it much longer. He snatched up his shirt.

"I'm sorry. I have to get out of here."

"What's wrong?"

The air shifted behind him, as if Landry had reached for him. Saber sprinted for the door. He couldn't slow. If Landry touched him, Saber would change. There was something about the man. He called to Saber's other side, drawing out the beast. That couldn't happen. Saber was inside his car and halfway home before his heart rate slowed. Reality slammed down on him, knocking the wind from his lungs. He'd just fucked up the best thing to ever happen to him. Goddamn it.

LANDRY: *We're both adults. All you have to do is tell me what I did wrong.*

LANDRY: *Or you could tell me to get lost.*

LANDRY: *Never mind. Lose my number.*

SABER: *I'm sorry. You make me feel things no one else ever has. I panicked.*

Landry: *Don't care. I gave you a few chances to explain. You ignored me. I don't play games.*

Saber: *I'm explaining now. Please just see me.*

Landry: *Lose my number or I'll block you.*

It took every ounce of Landry's willpower not to check his phone again as he dressed for work. Still, his gaze slid toward the dresser, where his ruined sheets sat. He couldn't explain why he'd washed them and folded them before leaving them in his line of sight. Maybe it was a combination of never seeing sheets shredded like that during a sexual encounter and knowing he'd driven Saber to show that much passion. Not that it changed anything. Saber had blown his mind and then booked ass before Landry came down from his high. The fucker. Landry had made his way through all the emotions. At first, he'd been confused. Then, he'd been hurt. Now, he was just pissed and done. Landry liked Saber, but he wasn't desperate for anyone's dick. They were over.

By the time Landry made it halfway through the

day and back to the station, he'd almost convinced himself it was true. Until he spotted Saber leaning against the front counter, flirting with Wendy, the girl who answered the phones. Of course he fucking was. The douche. Landry tore his gaze away from the ragged jeans cupping Saber's perfect ass. While holding his head high, he tried sneaking by without being notice. He barely made it two steps before Saber's head whipped around and his gorgeous blue gaze landed on Landry, pinning him in place.

"There he is. Thanks for your help," Saber said, sounding absent as he walked away from Wendy.

Landry rolled his eyes and started away. There was no law that said he had to speak to Saber just because the man had shown. Before Landry could make a clean getaway, a bouquet of wild flowers appeared in front of Landry. Landry ran his tongue over his teeth, fighting all the hate-filled words that rushed to his tongue. He didn't take the flowers.

"Please accept them, Landry. I'm sorry."

Against his will, Landry's gaze slid Saber's way. The temptation to cock punch him was real. "Why?"

Saber looked confused—like he was being set up. "Because I bought them for you."

Landry pinned the man in place with his stare. "No. Why should I forgive you?"

The cocky smile Landry loved and hated spread across Saber's face. "Because I'm an idiot and you knew that before you went out with me."

"I don't have time for this." He tried stepping around Saber.

Saber countered his every move. "Also, I'm an idiot who really, really cares about you."

An ugly-sounding snort escaped Landry. "You care so much you ran out on me without a single explanation and then ignored my calls and texts. Take this personally: go fuck yourself."

Saber dropped to his knees and held out the flowers. "Please forgive me. I'm stupid and I do stupid shit."

Landry stared down at Saber, speechless. Horror and the desire to laugh pulled him in different directions. No one had ever humbled themselves for Landry. He'd damned sure never seen anyone go so far in front of a station filled with over-the-top manly cops. Landry could feel the eyes upon them. He tried pulling Saber to his feet. Jesus, the guy was like trying to lift a truck when he decided he wouldn't be budged.

"Get up, Saber."

Saber shook his head. "Nope. Not until you tell me I'm forgiven."

A loud sigh escaped Landry. "You're such a pain in my ass."

"A loveable pain," Saber said, blinking like he was trying to be cute.

Landry made a helpless gesture. "So you just want me to lie and say you're forgiven, then you'll leave?"

"Nope," Saber said, obviously relishing his power to keep Landry trapped in this embarrassing situation. "Tell me you'll go to lunch with me and I'll get up."

A growl rose in Landry's throat. "Fine. For fuck's sake. Get up and I'll go to lunch with you."

"And you'll take my flowers."

"And I'll take your fucking flowers," Landry said, losing his temper.

Saber's triumphant smile made Landry want to take it back. Saber shot to his feet, looking like a man who hadn't just shown his ass in a police station. He slung his arm over Landry's shoulders and steered him toward the door. "Where we headed, babe? I'll take you anywhere you want to go." He passed the flowers Landry's way. Landry considered hitting Saber with them as his fingers closed around the bouquet.

"Someplace close by so this is over with quickly."

Landry spotted Saber's car in a nearby parking spot, making him wonder how he'd missed it coming in.

Saber opened the passenger-side door. "How about a picnic in my car, then?"

The sight of a small cooler on the floor made Landry realize this had been Saber's plan all along. He fought a growl. Saber always made him so damn crazy. It was like the man knew he could have whatever he wanted. Landry didn't want to be added to that list. He needed to be special. Saber already had too much of everything. Landry plopped down in the seat like a petulant child. Just because he'd agreed to this didn't mean he had to give Saber the satisfaction of enjoying it.

After closing the door, Saber circled the car and jumped behind the wheel. Landry quickly buckled his seatbelt when he realized Saber didn't intend to stay there. He backed from the parking spot and headed for a nearby parking garage where they weren't in the beating down sun. Landry counted to one hundred, trying to control his anger. Saber put the car back in park. Before Landry could take off his seatbelt, Saber was there. His mouth covered Landry's. Landry bit him. Saber moaned. The sound punched Landry in the chest.

Saber licked Landry's bottom lip. "I'm sorry," he

whispered against Landry's lips. "You unhinge me. I don't know how to handle it." He licked Landry again.

Landry's hand found Saber's hair. Instead of tugging him away, the way he told himself he would, his fingers tightened on the soft locks. He pulled the man closer. Their tongues met. Softly at first, seeking. Heat exploded through their kiss. Landry fought to get as close as possible. "You're not really forgiven," Landry said as he changed angles.

"I wouldn't expect anything less." Saber untucked Landry's shirt as he made the claim. His palm collided with Landry's erection. Landry sucked in a breath. Saber was too much. He always overwhelmed all of Landry's senses, making him nuts. "Goddamn. You look sexy in uniform. It makes it hard to keep my hands to myself." Landry tilted his chin up to give Saber better access to his throat. Saber shifted onto his knees. The man felt like he was everywhere. A chuckle unexpectedly rose in Landry's throat. Saber sat back. His offended expression made Landry laugh harder.

"You just got on your knees," Landry said between peals of laughter. "At my job. In front of everyone."

Saber nodded. His serious expression never wavered. "There's nothing I wouldn't do for you."

Landry's laughter died away. He brushed Saber's cheek with his fingertips before hauling the man toward him. "Regretting you never gets old," Landry whispered as their lips met. It was the most honest confession Landry could think to give Saber. He already knew Saber would pull something else before long. Landry would be right here, waiting to forgive him for it.

FIVE

SABER: COME STAY WITH ME TONIGHT. NO SEX. *Just cuddles. I want to fall asleep with you.*

Landry: *This sounds like a trap, but I'm still in.*

LANDRY: *The just sleeping thing was amazing. I can't remember the last time I had no trouble getting up before the sun.*

Saber: *Good. Let's do it again tonight.*

Landry: *I'll be there.*

SABER: *I heard on the radio a cop was shot today. Are you okay?*

Landry: *Wasn't me. I'm good. Bullet bounced and grazed his arm. Everyone is fine.*

Saber: *Damn. I never expected to worry this much. Be safe.*

Landry: *Always.*

———

LANDRY: *I'm off tomorrow. Come see me.*

Saber: *The second I'm off, I'll be there.*

Landry: *Plan to stay the night.*

Saber: *Sounds good.*

Landry: *Don't plan on sleeping.*

Saber: *Okay.*

Saber's text might've said okay, but his mind was in panic mode. He'd never wanted anyone more than he craved Landry. It was a sickness eating away at his brain all hours of the day. Each time he got close to making a move, his body tried to transform with no input from Saber.

He wasn't unsatisfied with their relationship. In fact, even without the sex, Saber had never been happier. Each time he curled up with Landry at night, everything felt right. He wanted to brush the back of his knuckles down Landry's jaw and watch him sleep for the rest of his life. His heart swelled every time Landry snuggled closer, seeking Saber even in his dreams.

Landry wouldn't stay on hold forever. Eventually, he'd question his worth, wondering why he wasn't good enough to fuck. In Landry's shoes, Saber would feel the same. There were only so many excuses Saber could make. All Saber knew for sure was he couldn't let Landry go.

Landry reached above his head for something on the top shelf in the cabinet. Saber spent a second watching the man's ass before he lost the battle against himself. His palms slid across Landry's hips. He drew the man back against him. Saber's heart swelled as his arms closed around Landry. His lips automatically sought the side of Landry's neck. He inhaled Landry's scent.

"*Mhmm*. This is really what I want to eat right here."

He felt the vibration of Landry's chuckle against his lips. "You say that now. In fifteen minutes, you'll be telling me you're hungry again."

Saber found the edge of Landry's shirt and dove beneath. Bare, hot skin tempted his fingertips to explore. He tried shoving his hand inside Landry's jeans, but while buttoned, they were too tight. Landry squirmed as Saber's fingers wiggled near his hipbone. Saber did it again and Landry tried to get it away.

"Oh my god. You're ticklish right there."

Landry tried harder to get away at the accusation. "I don't know what you're talking about."

Saber dug his fingers in to prove a point. Landry stiffened in his arms and fought him. A loud bark of laughter escaped Saber. "You are. Oh, I know what I'm doing later."

"I do too. You're eating and then going to bed."

"Yep," Saber said, making the "p" pop. "Where I'll be tickling you." He pulled his fingers out of Landry's jeans and backed away. "Tell me what I need to do to help."

Landry turned in a slow circle and eyed the kitchen. He pointed at a set of cabinet doors behind Saber. "Grab the big pot out of that cabinet, please?"

Saber turned to do as directed. Landry collided with Saber's back, pinning him against the counter. "Two can play at this game, you know," Landry said before his teeth sank into Saber's earlobe. His hands found their way beneath Saber's shirt. Saber went hard. A pant escaped him. Landry's lips skimmed

Saber's throat before his mouth found the spot where Saber's neck and shoulder met. He bit Saber again. Landry's hands slid up Saber's body until his fingertips collided with Saber's hardened nipples. He pinched them. Saber sucked in a breath. Landry's hands moved south again. He tried the same move as Saber had, attempting to get his fingers inside Saber's jeans. Landry didn't make it any deeper than Saber had. Landry spoke against Saber's throat, making Saber's dick even harder. "Be careful what threats you make. I own handcuffs. Once I have you at my mercy, I can do anything. Any promises you make good on might be the difference between pleasure and pain when I have you chained to the bed."

Saber almost came right then. A shiver ran through him. A drop of pre-cum sneaked out. "I like pleasure and pain, so I guess we'll see."

Landry fingers encircled Saber's throat. He urged Saber's head back until he could capture Saber's lips. With Saber held at an awkward angle and his mouth busy, Landry took advantage. His grip tightened on Saber's throat, distracting him just long enough for Landry have him by the cock. Saber's entire body jerked as Landry squeezed his erection. It was the first time Landry had ever touched his dick because Saber's body always tried to shift into tiger mode when Landry got too close.

"I could get you off right now, but I won't."

Oh, he was about to whether he planned it or not. Saber's dick hadn't had this much attention in months. Saber couldn't control it.

"Food first. Get that pot." Landry nipped at Saber's bottom lip as he made the demand before finally releasing him.

Saber gasped for air as he dug around for the big pot. His mind was a mess. He wanted Landry. Bad. But there was a real risk he'd turn. That would definitely ruin Landry's night.

Saber tried focusing on one thing at a time. He set the pot on the stove. "What are you making, anyhow?"

"It's an old family recipe from my mom's side of the family," Landry said, picking up a faded and old-looking sheet of paper from the counter. The paper slipped to the floor. "Shit," Landry cursed under his breath as he bent and scooped up the paper. Saber reached for it too. Landry stood before Saber could get out of the way. His head collided with Saber's mouth—hard. Saber slapped a hand to his mouth, tasting blood. He licked at his lip, using the antiseptic in his saliva to heal his split lip before

Landry saw. Saber couldn't risk Landry seeing him heal. Landry cupped his head with both hands without ever releasing the paper, obviously hurt from coming into contact with Saber's overly hard jaw. Saber tried prying his hands away to see.

"Are you okay? Let me look." Landry cursed as he gave in, letting Saber inspect him for wounds. Saber massaged Landry's head, finding a growing knot. He kissed it. "Oh, baby. I'm so sorry. Are you okay?"

Landry nodded and met his gaze. "It's my fault. Are you okay? Did I bust your lip?" He set the recipe on the counter before moving in close to check Saber for cuts. Landry went as far as to gently pull Saber's bottom lip down, ensuring his teeth hadn't cut into it. "Have you always had this scar on your lip? I swear I've stared at your mouth dozens of times and never noticed."

Saber started to laugh off Landry's claim. Weres don't scar. Unless... holy shit. "What scar?"

Landry fingered the exact spot where Landry had busted his lip. Desperation had him searching for any shiny surface to see his reflection. Saber snatched up the toaster and looked at his mouth. There it was—a scar from their impact. He set the toaster aside and stared at Landry. Every encounter they'd had and every extreme emotion he'd experienced since meeting Landry came together in his mind. Weres only scarred when marked by their mates. Fuck his life. Landry was his fated mate.

"I have to go."

Landry's expression snapped closed. "What?"

Saber headed for the door. He didn't look back. He couldn't. "I have to go." They were the only words that would come.

"Oh. We're doing this again."

Even Landry's dry words didn't stop him. He couldn't run away fast enough. Landry was human. This wasn't good. He'd never understand Saber being a tiger. In fact, as the front door closed behind him and Saber ran for his bike, he'd go as far as to say he was fucked. This was one thing he had no fucking clue how to explain.

FOR A FULL MINUTE Landry stared at the door Saber disappeared through, expecting him to come back and say it was all a joke. Just like last time, not only did Saber not return, Landry was left wondering what he'd done. Once reality set in and Landry accepted Saber wouldn't return, the anger set in. Saber was gone. Again. Landry had never considered himself an unforgiving person, but he didn't know if he could deal with this again. This time, it was best if Saber didn't return.

Landry sat at the kitchen table and stared at the ingredients spread throughout the room. He'd planned a nice night. Saber had a habit of ruining nice things. Why did Landry put up with so much bullshit? Saber was gorgeous, fun, and perfect in a lot of ways. But was he worth this hurt and anger boiling in Landry's gut? Maybe Landry needed a reminder that Saber wasn't the only man in the world. While stuck on autopilot, Landry headed for the living room. He found his phone and scrolled through his contacts. Landry hardened his heart with each passing second. He hadn't been in a relationship in a long time. Drama and Landry weren't friends. Saber was a reminder of all the reasons why. There was no reason for him to feel guilty. Saber was the one who left.

Landry: *What are you doing tonight?*

Nolan: *Hanging at the house. Why?*

Landry: *I'm cooking my grandmother's chicken and dumplings. Interested?*

Nolan: *I ran into Shepherd a few days ago. He*

said you're dating a biker. I thought that was a little interesting.

Fucking Shepherd. He loved his brother, but he had a big mouth.

Landry: *Is that a no?*

Nolan: *I like you, Landry. Always have. I like you too much to come over when you're dating someone else.*

Landry's fingers hovered over the face of his phone. He wanted to claim he wasn't seeing anyone. Saber had walked out on him, for fuck's sake. That made him single. Right? Landry tossed the phone onto the couch and scrubbed his hands through his hair. Aggravation owned him. Saber didn't deserve his loyalty. The guy obviously felt none toward Landry. Landry stared at the wall, trying not to feel anything. Saber's face wouldn't leave his head. He was keeping something from Landry. Landry could feel it in his bones. Maybe Saber really was a drug dealer. He'd never seen him work. A snort escaped Landry. Maybe he was just trying to make himself feel like it wasn't his fault Saber obviously didn't want him. His phone vibrated across the maroon-colored cushion. Landry watched it happen. His interest in talking to anyone fled. Instead, he made his way back to the kitchen. After tossing all the uncooked food, Landry dug a bottle of Jack from the freezer and headed for his bedroom. If he was doomed to spend the rest of his life alone, he may well get used to drinking in his empty bed.

BACKWOODS RIBS 'N More was dead for the usual lunchtime rush. Saber chose a table in Zara's section, hoping to catch her in between customers. The slow business let her sit with him instead. Saber stared at the red-haired girl he'd grown up with as she filled the chair beside him. They'd been cubs together, playing in the same overgrown pools and catching prey. There'd only ever been one other person who knew him as well as Zara, and she was dead. Zara had been Saber's sister Sierra's best friend. When Saber and Sierra had moved to New Orleans, Zara had tagged along. So too had Zara's brother, Tao. Tao had fallen in love with Sierra. Their relationship had been nothing but drama, passion, and jealousy. All the way up until the day Tao killed her. Bonds had been made and broken that day.

"You look good," Zara said as she tucked Saber's hair behind his ear.

A chuckle escaped him. "Liar."

Zara smiled. Her light green eyes were sad for a moment. Her smile fell, and she dropped her hand. "Would you rather I tell you that you look like shit?"

Saber shrugged. "It's true. At least I know it." He took her hand and kissed the back. Saber didn't release her. "On the other hand, you look beautiful. How are you holding up?"

A sad smile passed over Zara's features before slipping away. "For a moment, I was good when I woke up this morning. Then, I caught a glimpse of the calendar and it fled."

He got it. Today marked a year since they'd lost everything. First, Zara had found Sierra's lifeless body, and then she'd watched as Tao had been put to death for his crime. "It's not your fault." They were the same words Saber had given her a million times since that day. No matter how true they were, they also changed nothing. "I just wanted to stop by and check on you."

Zara squeezed his hand. "Really, Saber. I'm good. All things aside, I've been getting by. In fact, I've been in touch with my parents, and I'm thinking of returning home. Mom has—believe or not—stopped blaming me for wanting to move here. Now she thinks I needed to see more of the world before settling down."

A bark of laughter escaped Saber. "You know she probably already has a nice young man picked out for you."

"Meh," Zara said with a shrug. "Maybe I need a nice young man. I'm not getting any younger and it's not like there are any of our kind around these parts. I can't settle down with a human."

A shot of pain hit Saber in the chest. "Actually, I wanted to tell—" The scent of the jungle filled his nose. Saber turned his head, searching for the source. Landry stood near the door, holding a takeout order. Their gazes met and held. Landry's closed expression sank in, making Saber realize how bad things looked... again. He dropped Zara's hand. It was too late. The damage was done. Landry turned away and pushed through the door, leaving him behind.

"Fuck."

"Who was that?"

At Zara's question, a loud sigh escaped Saber. "My fated mate."

"He's human." There was no judgment in Zara's voice, only surprise.

Saber scrubbed his hands through his hair, considering tearing it from the roots. "Yeah."

Her gaze moved over his face. "And unclaimed."

"Yep."

"Fuck."

Saber snorted. "That pretty much sums it up."

She shoved at his shoulder. "Go after him. There's no one filled with more wrathful jealousy than an unclaimed tiger mate."

That was all the permission Saber needed. He hurried for the door and overcame Landry as he opened the door to his car. All thoughts of running away disappeared. "Landry, hold up. It's not what you think."

Landry spun on him, catching Saber off guard with his fury. "It's never what I think, right?" He visibly took a breath, as if trying to calm himself. "Not that it matters. I think you made your position clear by running out on me last night. I guess I know why now."

Saber scrambled to make things right. "She's my sister's best friend. *Was* my sister's best friend," Saber said, correcting himself. "Today, it's been a year since Sierra died and Zara is the one who found her. There is nothing going on between us other than commiserating over our loss."

Landry pinched the spot between his eyes before meeting Saber's stare again. "You make me crazy, Saber. I've never been a jealous person. It's like there's something wrong with us. You keep saying it's not me, but I kind of think it is, because you keep running away and I keep finding you with women."

"Zara is only a friend. I swear."

"And I believe that," Landry said, sounding like it was true. "But that doesn't change my reaction to seeing you with someone else, especially after yesterday. I'm tired of your secrets. It's exhausting trying to figure out if you're hiding something or if you just don't want me. This isn't me. I'm not jealous or insecure, except with you." He made a helpless gesture. "Being with someone is supposed to feel good. We just feel... I don't know—like we're missing something that would make me feel secure. I can't explain it. It's like I don't feel like I'm good enough to keep you. You keep disappearing like you're not really mine, so I'm waiting on the other shoe to drop. I don't like myself with you. You make me question my worth."

Saber rushed to make it right. "It's not your fault." It really wasn't. Until Landry was claimed, he would always feel like part of him was missing. Every day, it would get worse, and it was all Saber's fault, because he'd chased the man, knowing he was human. It was Evan all over again, with Saber pursuing a man out of his reach. That didn't mean he'd stop. He rubbed Landry's arms, trying to comfort him. When Landry let it go on, Saber shifted closer. "Give me another chance."

There was so much pain in Landry's eyes, it was choking Saber. "I'm tired of being angry, confused, and hurt. How many chances do you need? I'm running on empty."

It wouldn't get better if Landry walked away. They were fated. The longing would double if they were apart. "Just one more. See me tonight. Let me come over when you get off work. Seriously, I can make this better."

A snort escaped Landry. "Is this one more blow job to distract me while you plot your getaway?"

Saber moved even closer until their bodies met. His gaze never wavered from Landry's. "Just believe in me one more time. I panicked because you scare the hell out of me, but I'm not giving up. I'm sorry for everything. Don't shut me out. Not yet."

Landry's shoulders fell, and Saber smelled victory. "Why can't I walk away from you?"

"Because you know I feel the same," Saber said, trying to make him understand something he couldn't. Not yet. Not until he knew the truth. "You feel me when you look at me. This is real. You don't walk away from what's real that easy."

Landry's gaze moved over Saber's face. He could feel Landry's hunger. "I'm sorry I overreacted."

Saber shook his head. "You didn't. I would've done the same. You're mine. If I'd seen you holding someone else's hand, it would've been worse. They would've been missing an arm."

Landry chuckled. Saber was one hundred fucking percent serious. No one touched what belonged to him. Landry didn't understand jealousy like a dominant tiger. Saber's gums itched as the beast inside stirred—restless and angry at the idea of anyone touching his mate. He had to find Evan. He was the only person Saber had ever felt like he could talk to, even if it wasn't about anything heavy. It was time to apologize and get back his friend. Saber needed advice. He didn't know how to handle this, but he had to find a way. Landry deserved that much.

SIX

SABER BLINKED AT THE "CLOSED" SIGN IN confusion. Baptiste's Voodoo Shop was never closed. But now, on the day of Saber's need, he was closed. Saber glanced around, trying to decide what to do. He spotted the uber sexy guy who owned the vintage dress shop across the street. Saber had tried many times to get the dark-haired man's number. Keegan wasn't having it. That small connection was all he needed, though.

"Hey, Keegan. Do you know why Baptiste's place is closed?"

The gorgeous shop owner turned from hosing down the outside of his building to focus on Saber. His sexy smile and stunning eyes didn't have the same effect as they had in the past. Saber only noticed the man's beauty in a detached way now. No one was sexier than Landry. "Hey, Saber. Yeah. They had a small fire. Baptiste said he planned to use the opportunity to stay with his friend Jonathan while the building was repaired."

Great. Saber would have to visit the king and grovel in front of the whole fucking clan. It was for Landry, Saber reminded himself. "Thanks. See you later."

After tossing him a small wave, Keegan went back to cleaning. Saber straddled his bike and took a deep breath. The last time he'd gone to Jonathan's, he'd been looking for Risk. Risk had been too busy to help. Hopefully, Baptiste wouldn't be too busy to see him. Things with Landry would never be right if Saber couldn't claim him. Fuck. Everything was a mess. He'd never expected to find his mate. Saber definitely hadn't been looking. But when Saber was with Landry, everything felt right. Everything had seemed so simple at first. Landry turned him on and made him happy. Saber never expected that to lead to him having to find a way to explain he wasn't human. Landry had already marked him. It had been an accident, but it didn't matter. The results were the same. Landry was his.

At Jonathan's, everything was quiet. The

sprawling mansion where the king lived was in the center of a massive plot of land at the edge of a huge nature preserve. It was the perfect spot to hide a clan of vampires. It was also a great place for Evan to play. After ringing the doorbell, Saber shifted nervously from one foot to the other. If Baptiste or Evan refused to accept his apology, his life was over. They were probably the only people who could help him. By the time Lire answered, Saber thought he'd be sick.

The demon eyed him. His long, dark hair hung in his face. "Jonathan is sleeping."

Saber nodded. Fuck, he hadn't considered the time. "I was told Baptiste is here." He knew Baptiste rarely slept during the day since he had a shop to run and his mates didn't need sleep.

"All the vamps are in bed."

Double fuck. "Is Evan around?"

Lire waved Saber inside. "Evan's out back with Tamil."

"Who the hell is Tamil?" He hadn't meant to sound so hostile. It was his nerves talking.

As Lire led the way to the back door, he answered over his shoulder. "He's Risk's blood mate."

"Risk has a mate? Damn. I've been out of the

loop." He hadn't felt quite as welcome since the thing with Evan, and the last time he'd seen Risk, the man had been busy doing something for the king.

Lire stopped and faced Saber. "Oh, which reminds me. Tam is very sweet and sensitive. That's why we keep him away from strangers. If you upset him, I'll rip you open and feed you your insides, 'kay?" He opened the door. "Have fun with the boys."

Saber stared at Lire without blinking. It was the friendliest-sounding threat he'd ever received, yet Saber didn't doubt the demon for a second. As the seventh son of Asmodeus, he was an extremely powerful being. The entire incident made him curious as hell. He was somewhat excited to meet Tamil now. Anyone who secured the loyalty of someone like Lire had to be interesting. Plus, Saber was a bit twisted. Threats merely turned him on.

With a sharp nod, Saber acknowledged Lire's warning. "Duly noted. It was good to see you." Saber moved past Lire and headed for the backyard.

Two figures sat under a tree on either side of a cauldron, which Saber found funny. He knew Evan was in the process of learning magic, but the use of an actual cauldron struck him as hilarious. He recognized Evan's dark hair right away. The guy with his back to Saber had curly blond hair and was much smaller than Evan. Saber's steps slowed as he got close enough to hear their conversation.

"A kiss for luck. Hmmm. At the same time, then? You do that side and I'll do this one," the blond said, pointing to opposite sides of a white and pink rose.

Evan's bright smile had Saber's lips curving upward. "Sounds good. One. Two. Three. Go." They both leaned forward and kissed the rose. A loud laugh escaped them as they dropped the flower in the cauldron. They sounded so much like kids, it was fun to watch.

"Okay. Bamboo and clover next." At Evan's instruction, the blond dumped a few more items in.

"What are the two of you up to?" At Saber's question, Evan's gaze jerked his way. The blond didn't immediately turn. Instead, he picked up a tiny doll in a blue dress and tucked it beneath the tail of his shirt before turning. As his gaze landed on Saber, Saber fought the urge to suck in a breath. He didn't think he'd ever been in the presence of such pure innocence.

Evan reached across the cauldron and set a hand on Tamil as if attempting to keep him calm. He shifted positions, giving Saber the impression Evan was trying to place himself bodily between Saber and Tamil without drawing attention to the fact.

"Hey, Saber. We're making a luck potion."

Saber moved to join them, dropping down in an empty spot at the edge of the cauldron. He peeked inside the pot. He didn't know if their spell would work, but it smelled pretty good—like a fresh garden. Saber focused on Tamil. "Hi. I'm Saber."

Sky-blue eyes shifted his way. "I'm Tamil."

Damn. His small, sweet voice matched the rest of him. "Don't let me interrupt. I just came to visit, but we can chat while you two work." In fact, Saber preferred for everyone to have something splitting their attention while he poured out his heart.

Tamil nodded and stirred the mixture. "It's okay. I won't look at you."

At Tamil's odd comment, Saber found himself staring at the boy. "What?"

"You're uncomfortable, so I won't look at you."

Oh, he was too sweet. "It's not because you're looking at me. I need to apologize to Evan and I'm not used to saying I'm sorry."

"You shouldn't worry about talking to Evan. He's very forgiving."

Evan chuckled. "That depends if the apology is genuine."

"It is," Saber said, keeping his voice level. This was too important to fuck up. "You didn't deserve to have someone like me come around. I didn't have anything to offer, and I knew it." Both men stopped what they were doing and looked his way. His discomfort doubled. He didn't let that stop him. "The thing is, I knew you weren't meant for me, and —honestly—that was part of the appeal. I wasn't looking for a mate. But now, I've found him, and things are different."

"You found your mate? That's nice," Tamil said, sounding genuine. "I hope that means you won't try kissing mine again."

Tamil's statement brought Saber up short. "What?"

"The last time you were here," Tamil explained. "You tried kissing Risk. I was sitting over there when it happened," he said, pointing toward a nearby willow tree.

To his surprise, heat blossomed in his cheeks. "Oh, um, I guess I owe you an apology too. Damn." He was really winning at life today.

Tamil shook his head. He looked ridiculously earnest. Saber couldn't look away from him. "No. Risk is one of those people who makes people want to kiss him. It's kind of flattering that he could've chosen you, but he didn't. You're a lot better in every way than I am."

"That's not true," Saber spat. Even he didn't know why he had to disabuse Tamil of that thought, but he didn't like knowing the man believed something like that. "Just ask Evan. I'm a terrible person."

Evan looked like a deer caught in headlights when they looked his way. "Um... terrible is going a bit far. Maybe more like thoughtless of other people's feelings. Before I came to your cabin that night, I thought you were pretty great. I just wanted to talk because I needed a friend. It never occurred to me you might be using me until that moment."

Guilt ate at Saber. He didn't like knowing someone as amazing as Evan thought badly of him. "When I came by the shop—the day Baptiste cursed me—I came to apologize, but Baptiste wouldn't let me see you. I should've told you that you scared the hell out of me, because no one else had ever made me consider settling down before you. Then, I just totally fucked up everything. I'm really good at that, actually."

"Baptiste cursed you?" Tamil asked, obviously trying to keep up.

"No," Evan said with a laugh before Saber could answer. "He sprayed him with glass cleaner."

"No. He actually cursed me," Saber argued. Honestly, he was a bit offended Baptiste had obviously lied to Evan about what happened.

A line appeared between Evan's brows. "I was there. Baptiste had me hidden behind a wall of magic. He sprayed you with glass cleaner."

Saber shook his head, confused. "But that doesn't make sense."

Tamil reached for him.

Saber backed away out of habit. He was a tiger. People didn't touch him unless he allowed it. The flash of hurt that crossed Tamil's features at his over-the-top reaction made Saber's chest hurt.

Tamil dropped his gaze to his lap and twisted the doll hiding beneath his shirt. "I'm sorry. Sometimes I forget that people don't like my touch."

Evan shot him a look that would've flayed him alive if looks killed. "Tamil can read magic." Evan didn't add "dumbass" to the end of his sentence, but Saber got the feeling it was understood.

Saber rushed to fix it. "I'm a weretiger. It was an instinctive reaction from living in the wild. It's okay if you touch me."

This time, Tamil didn't look his way as he

reached for Saber. He still looked worried Saber didn't want him nearby. Saber shifted closer, hoping the move proved he wasn't bothered by Tamil's touch. Tamil's warm palm landed on Saber's forearm before falling away. "Jonathan cursed you."

"What?"

"You mean you really are cursed?" Evan asked at the same time.

Saber ignored Evan's question. He couldn't look away from Tamil. "Are you being serious? Jonathan cursed me? That asshole."

Tamil glanced his way and looked away just as quickly. He scratched the bridge of his nose, looking uncomfortable as fuck. "Um, I can check again. It's possible I'm wrong."

Saber moved even closer until their thighs nearly touched. "Please?" He held his arm out to Tamil.

Tamil sneaked another quick glance his way before setting his hand on Saber's arm. This time, he didn't pull away. Warmth moved up Saber's arm toward his chest. He tried not to panic. The world tilted. For a moment, Saber stared at the way his feet dangled a foot off the ground before it broke through his brain that he really was hanging a foot off the ground.

"Why are you touching my mate?"

Saber glanced over his shoulder, catching sight of Risk. His eyes glowed and his fangs were bared. Until that moment—held in one hand by the back of his neck like a rag doll—Saber had never realized how terrifying it was to be in a vampire's bad graces.

"Hey, baby." Tamil sounded doubly sweet and happy to see Risk as if Saber wasn't an inch from losing his life. "He wasn't touching me. I was touching him."

Saber's eyes fell closed. He didn't see how that was helping.

Risk's hold slackened a hair. "Are you okay, sweets?"

Saber kept glancing between them. Tamil was completely calm while Saber's life was in Risk's hands.

Tamil nodded. "Jonathan cursed him, but it's okay. I fixed him."

"You did?" Saber's happiness outweighed his fear.

Risk set Saber on his feet. His hard stare warned Saber not to move as he helped Tamil to his feet. "That was nice of you, baby. Why don't we go hang out in our hiding spot while Evan talks to Saber? We can see them from there," Risk added with a definite growl, proving Saber wasn't completely off his shit list.

Tamil's smile was adorable. Saber was almost jealous as Risk brushed his lips across Tamil's. The boy reminded him a lot of Evan, except there was something different about him—dark and damaged. Tamil moved to Evan's side. He bent and kissed Evan's cheek. "I'll come back later."

Without looking back, Risk took Tamil's hand and led him away. Before they were out of earshot, Tamil's whisper reached him. "What did he do to Evan? Should I have left him cursed?"

"Oh, boy," Risk said, as if gearing up to tell a sordid tale.

Saber's eyes fell closed. If he ever got out of this shit, he wasn't messing with this clan any longer. He would head back to his plot of land on the edge of werewolf country and refuse to budge.

"So you've really been cursed this whole time. That's... wow."

Saber focused on Evan. "Yep."

"Now you've found your mate. Is that the only reason you came to apologize? To get the curse lifted?"

After dropping back onto the ground across from Evan, Saber held the man's stare. "No. Like I said, I wanted to apologize the day Baptiste—apparently—sprayed me with glass cleaner. I really am sorry. It was never my intention to hurt you. You're right. We were friends. I don't want to lose that."

Evan smiled and went back to stirring his potion. "Don't worry. I don't hold grudges. That night, when I showed up at your cabin, my life was in shambles. I just needed... I don't know. Someone to tell me I wasn't a loser, I guess." Evan shrugged. "The way I found you, it was just getting kicked while down, I suppose. That was months ago, though. A lot has changed."

Saber looked around, trying to think of a way to move past their past. "I see that. Like Risk and Tamil. I didn't even know Risk had a mate. When did that happen? And what's wrong with him?"

"Nothing is wrong with him," Evan snapped, looking outraged. "He's amazing and sweet, and he deserves so much better than having you ask what's wrong with him. Tamil spent years held against his will and tortured by a demon. You can't imagine—"

"Whoa," Saber said, holding up his hands. "I was joking. I meant what's wrong with him that he'd settle for Risk. Damn. You really don't think much of me, do you?"

Evan blew out a sigh. "I'm sorry. It's not you.

You've missed a bunch of stuff. I've become a bit sensitive about the Tamil topic. It's only recently I've been allowed to spend time alone with him." Evan rubbed his forehead. "It's a hot button topic around here."

Saber thought things over. It was possible he should've checked in sooner. Offered his help. "I can't believe Tamil was tortured. He's so nice. That's..." There were no words.

"Yeah." Evan brightened. "Tell me about your mate, though. What's his name?"

"Landry." Saber couldn't even say Landry's name without smiling. Evan looked interested and understanding. Saber's smile slipped away. "I'm scared shitless." The confession fell before Saber could stop it. He didn't have friends. Evan was the only person he could talk to. "He's human. How am I supposed to explain..." Saber motioned helplessly at their surroundings, "... all this? What if he runs away screaming? I would."

Evan scooped some potion into a vial and handed it to Saber. "Drink this."

Saber sniffed it. "Is it safe?"

"It might not work for its purpose," Evan said, obviously unconcerned. "If not, you'll have flowery breath."

With a shrug, Saber tossed back the potion. It tasted like he'd licked a flower bed. Since that wasn't the most disgusting thing he'd ever licked, he figured he'd live.

Evan's smile made the risk worthwhile. "May I borrow your phone?" Evan asked, sounding too excited for Saber to deny him. Saber unlocked it and passed it over. Evan scrolled around and then pressed the device to his ear. He chewed his bottom lip as he waited for his call to be answered. Saber couldn't look away. Maybe they'd found different mates, but Evan was still sexy. Saber heard someone answer, but he couldn't make out their words.

Evan chuckled. "Thank you for the compliment, but this is Evan. I just borrowed Saber's phone." That was interesting. It was obviously someone Saber knew. "Are you somewhere you can take down an address? Great." Saber listened as Evan rattled off the address to where they currently sat. "We, Saber's friends and I, are having a small get-together tonight. We would love to finally meet you." Evan nodded as he listened. A suspicion sneaked in. "Yes. I'm sitting here with him. He's apprehensive about you meeting us because we're weirdos. Saber thinks you'll run away screaming." Fuck. It *was* Landry. Saber tried reaching for the phone. Evan scrambled away. He kept talking. Saber didn't hear a word. His pulse beat loudly in his ears. Landry couldn't meet this clan. This was the king's home. If he ran, it would mean Saber had exposed not only their world but their king to humans. Saber went after Evan, determined to put a stop to this. Evan leapt, surprising the fuck out of Saber with the air he got. He scrambled up the tree. Evan had youth and obvious practice on his side. Before Saber could go after him, a hand landed on his shoulder, stopping him. He glanced over. His gaze landed on Jonathan. He was in full Nephilim mode. His eyes swirled like pots of leprechaun's gold.

"Leave him." At Jonathan's order, Saber's shoulders fell. Jonathan squeezed, and Saber didn't feel alone anymore. It was instant—like Jonathan took away the fear. "Goddess Celeste chose Landry for you. She'd never choose a weak man for this life. Let him meet us. If things go badly, we can scrub his memory and you can start over. That's better than telling him on your own and letting the chips fall where they may."

He knew Jonathan was right, but Saber was kind of pissed at everyone right now. "Helping me with this doesn't mean I'm not still angry with you about that curse."

One corner of Jonathan's mouth lifted. "It helped you find Landry, didn't it?"

Saber opened his mouth to argue, but Jonathan was right. He'd thought Landry was hot the first time he set eyes on him, but he wouldn't have pursued the man if he hadn't gone hard when Landry stopped him from falling over. "I feel certain I still have an argument here, but I'm too scared of Landry's reaction right now to think straight." It was actually worse than that. He knew Jonathan claimed they could wipe Landry's memories and he could start over, but fuck. Saber didn't want that. He didn't want Landry to go through that. Saber sure as fuck didn't want anyone taking their memories away from Landry. He wanted every night they'd spent on the water and every time Landry had fallen asleep in his arms to stay in Landry's head. Maybe Saber was an idiot. Possibly, Landry was crazy for wanting him. But for some screwed-up reason, Landry had chosen him, and Saber couldn't consider what it would be like to lose him. He'd find a way to stay with Landry, even if it meant he gave up his tiger side.

SEVEN

FOLLOWING THE DIRECTIONS ON HIS GPS, Landry ended up fifteen minutes outside of town and on the edge of a wildlife preserve. No amount of preparation would've been sufficient for his first glimpse of the house. After passing through an iron gate, he wound his way down the driveway toward the sprawling mansion. The gigantic brick home was surrounded by gorgeous landscaping. Tons of flowers and trees, including a huge willow whose branches draped all the way to the ground accented the property. The air felt strange. It made the hair stand on Landry's arms, as if he'd passed through an invisible wall of electricity.

Saber's motorcycle was the only vehicle he spotted. Landry parked beside it and made his way to the front door. His nerves frayed as he pushed the button, ringing the doorbell. He was already worried Saber's friends wouldn't like him before he saw how out of his league he was, but now. Landry shook his head. No way would these people like him.

The front door opened, and Landry stared into the face of the most adorable man he'd ever seen. Dark hair and blue eyes. He looked young, nice, and over enthusiastic. Before he spoke a word, Landry already knew this was the same man he'd spoken to on the phone.

"Evan?"

He looked twice as happy when he nodded. "And you're Landry," he said with certainty. He hopped forward and hugged Landry before Landry knew it would happen. A chuckle escaped him over Evan's enthusiasm. He seemed sweet. Landry couldn't picture him being friends with Saber. "Come on," Evan said, grabbing his hand and hauling him inside. "Everyone is out back. They can't wait to meet you." Evan practically dragged him through the house as he rattled on. The boy was surprisingly strong. "Well, not everyone. Jonathan, Cin, and Niall aren't outside yet. Not because they're not excited to meet you. At least I know Jonathan is. It's hard to tell with Niall because he's a little dark and moody. Don't worry, though. He doesn't bite. Well, he does, but I'm sure he won't bite you. I can't say the same for Faolan. He's the jokester of the bunch. Nothing he does surprises me. Oh, and I should warn you. Kallus and Lire won't shake hands. It's nothing personal. They just can't touch anyone other than their ma—husbands." Evan stopped at a set of French doors. "Which reminds me. I should also warn you about our throuples."

Landry had a hard time keeping up. Evan was a bit overwhelming. He'd dragged Landry through a gorgeous house so fast Landry had barely caught a glimpse. Evan also spoke faster than anyone Landry had ever met. "I'm sorry. What's a throuple?"

Evan took a breath—like he was taking a second to think how to explain or gearing up for another round of nonstop chatter. "Keep in mind, not everyone here is from here. Well, really no one here is from here. I'm the closest one, since I'm from Canada, but even still, that's not close. Compared to everyone else it is, but they have a different belief system. Their religion sometimes allows for more than one mate. I mean, spouse. So, Cin, Jonathan, and Niall. This is their house, by the way. They're married to each other." That was new, but Landry was cool with it.

"Okay."

Evan nodded. "Baptiste, Kallus, and Eirik are also married to each other. Baptiste is my person. You'll love him. Faolan, Dougal, and Lire are also together. They're Jonathan and Niall's security team, but they're so sweet, you won't be able to tell. I'm trying to think if I should warn you about anything else."

Landry watched as he tapped his chin and stared into space. He wanted to ask what Evan meant by saying Baptiste was his person. He hated to ask because they might never get outside and Landry wanted to see Saber. Landry opened his mouth to ask about Saber and Evan cut him off.

"Oh, you'll absolutely adore Tamil. He's my friend. You'll pick him out right away. He looks like a tiny angel. The moment you meet him, you'll instantly want to hug him, but don't. He's a little damaged and his husband will definitely rip your arms off. That's no way to start a party." Evan shrugged. "I think I've prepared you the best I can. If you get nervous, you can stick to my side. I promise no one will hurt you, even though some of the guys look a little scary. Saber would never let anything happen to you. Let's go." He grabbed Landry's hand again and took off, throwing open the French doors before leading Landry outside. There was a raging bonfire with several people gathered around. The backyard was even more beautiful than the front. There were more willow trees and flowers. The brush got thicker until finally becoming a forest along the property line.

Landry didn't have much time to enjoy the scenery. He scrambled along, trying to keep up with Evan's clipped pace as he dragged him over to the group. "Hey, everyone," Evan said, sounding bright. "This is Landry."

Everyone nodded or gave him a small wave. Evan was right. Some of them were a tad scary-looking. Mostly because they were massive. A few of the men looked like they belonged in a strong man competition. Evan was also right about Tamil. Landry picked him out right away, and he did look like a tiny angel.

Evan pointed at people and started naming names. The first was a man with long, dark hair that hung over his shoulders in waves. "This is Lire." Landry nodded at him, recalling the man didn't touch people.

"Nice to meet you."

"You, as well," Lire said.

Landry suppressed a chill. He had the most

seductive voice Landry had ever heard. It was almost musical—like he could bring a person to orgasm by his voice alone. Landry found his gaze skirting away to the next person. A gigantic man with amethyst eyes stood at Lire's side. Landry was fascinated. He'd never seen eyes like his, but there was something else about him. It was like good humor rolled off him in waves.

"Faolan?" Landry guessed.

The man nodded. His smile lit up the outdoors. "Aye. I see you've been warned."

A chuckle slipped from Landry's lips. Scottish. Landry loved it. Of course, the other man at Faolan's side gave it away with his kilt. "So this must be Dougal, then?"

"Aye," the blond beauty replied. Landry felt the man's extreme good looks and accent were what Evan truly should have warned him about. Goddamn. It was like the gene pool lotto had exploded in the backyard.

The tiny angel stood tucked beneath the arm of a dark-skinned man with amber eyes. Landry focused on the pair. "Tamil, I recognize from Evan's description, but I don't think Evan told me your name," he said, meeting the amber gaze.

"Risk," the man said, extending his free hand for Landry to shake.

Landry accepted, grateful to have one person welcoming him. "It's nice to meet you."

Before Landry could move on to the other people waiting to meet him, a silver-haired man with perfect features appeared from the shadows. He overcame Evan as if they were completely alone. Evan's feet left the ground as the man easily lifted him with one arm as their lips met. A smile tugged at the corners of Landry's mouth. At first glance, the new arrival appeared too old and stern for Evan, but it was obvious the hair color wasn't natural. Not to mention, no one rigid would openly kiss anyone as blatantly sexual as he did Evan. Jesus. Landry knew he should look away, but wow. He couldn't. Damn, he really wanted to find Saber. As if Saber heard his thoughts, he appeared from the same shadowy tree line as Evan's man. His face lit as his gaze landed on Landry. Landry's heart skipped a beat. Everyone else disappeared in Landry's eyes. It was like they were alone.

"Mine," Saber growled a half second before he overcame Landry. Landry had never been big into possessiveness, but Saber's was hot as hell. Their lips brushed before Saber bumped him with his nose lovingly. Landry found himself clinging to Saber's shirt. He'd never felt so much so fast with anyone, but he couldn't pretend he didn't, especially since Saber didn't hide the fact that he felt something too. "Sorry I was late. Bleidd and I were doing a security check. Have you met everyone?"

That was the second reference to security. Landry wondered who these people were that they needed so much protection. "Just about. I haven't met these three," he said, motioning toward the final three people to Risk's left, before waving a hand Evan's way. "Or Evan's man."

Evan pushed at the man's chest, laughing. "Sorry," he said, tossing Landry a blushing smile. "This is my husband, Bleidd."

"Charmed," Bleidd said without looking Landry's way. He was too busy with his forehead pressed to Evan's temple, trying to woo Evan into kissing him again. Landry's smile wouldn't abate. Evan struck Landry as the kind of person who deserved to have someone who couldn't keep their hands off him. He definitely needed someone to keep his mouth busy.

"I'm Baptiste."

Landry turned at the man's smooth voice. A blond man with two men flanking him stood waiting to shake Landry's hand. Landry accepted. "Nice to meet you."

Baptiste didn't release him immediately. His gaze moved over Landry's features as if searching for something. A frisson ran up Landry's arm. A smile broke out across Baptiste's face. "You have much goodness and light inside your heart. I'm glad to see it. These are my men, Kallus and Eirik."

Landry nodded at Kallus. The man's eyes were an electric blue. Almost unnatural. Landry had to tear his gaze away. When he focused on Eirik, his mind stuttered for a moment. "Oh. Evan didn't tell me he had a twin." He immediately felt like an ass for sounding like Evan should have warned him. "Sorry. He told me so much in such a short period of time, I guess I thought he would've mentioned that." He bit back a nervous laugh. They might be twins in looks, but that was where it ended. Eirik bled power. It was intimidating.

A loud, jovial laugh escaped Eirik, setting Landry at ease. "Evan is a talker."

"It's endearing," Landry said, incapable of not defending Evan, even though they'd just met.

"I like him," Baptiste said, directing his words at Saber. "He won't let anyone be disrespected. It makes sense your other half would carry that trait."

Landry blinked. He couldn't decide if Baptiste meant to compliment Landry or insult Saber. Saber gently tugged on Landry's hand, pulling his attention Saber's way. "Will you be okay if I leave you alone another minute or two? I need to run inside."

He was sweet. Landry carried a gun. "I'm good. Go do whatever you need. I'll be right here."

Saber kissed him again. As he pulled away, their gazes met. For a moment, Landry swore he could hear Saber's thoughts. Feel his feelings. The moment left him overwhelmed with emotion. He didn't understand what was happening between them. Then the moment was over, and Saber left him standing there. Landry blinked at his surroundings. Everyone was doing their own thing. Landry preferred that over everyone staring at him.

Evan sidled up next to him with Bleidd. "Everyone likes you. I can tell."

Landry glanced around again. He wasn't really feeling the love, but neither was anyone really shunning him. "They all seem nice." Landry glanced over to say more, but Bleidd had already reclaimed Evan's attention. This time, he had to look away. They were adorable, but he was starting to feel like a perv. He cast a glance around. Tamil caught his attention. Landry couldn't take his eyes off the blond. The way he looked at his husband with unwavering adoration had Landry mesmerized. He'd been a cop a long time. If there was anything Landry was an expert at, it was recognizing someone who'd survived a horrible trauma. Tamil had lived through something unspeakable. It was written in his every action. Yet he'd obviously found someone amazing. Someone who made him feel safe. Landry had to know more. Without thought, he moved closer. Tamil's sky-blue gaze flickered his way before sliding away. He looked nervous. Landry stopped a few feet away, hoping the man wouldn't feel intimidated.

"Hi."

Tamil peeked out at him from beneath his lashes and shuffled closer to his husband. "Hi."

Landry smiled. Tamil's voice was soft and sweet. Landry kept his tone low, hoping to set Tamil at ease. "Do you mind if I ask you a strange question?" Tamil shook his head and Landry motioned toward a doll that was somewhat hidden beneath the man's shirt. "Where did you get that doll?"

Tamil glanced down and gingerly untied the doll's dress from his belt loop. He held it out to Landry. "Risk made it for me."

Landry hesitated before taking it. Tamil's arm was covered in scars—like he'd been chewed on by a wild animal or wrapped in barbed wire. He forced his eyes away from the marks. After accepting the doll, Landry inspected it. Its body was small enough to fit in the palm of his hand and it was made of some sort of bandages or burlap. There was something about it. It was special in some way he couldn't define, but the tiny girl comforted him. Set him at ease. He handed it back. "Do you sell them?" Landry asked, directing his question at Risk. "I work with abused children sometimes. It would be amazing if I could carry something like that in my patrol car to give to kids who've been traumatized."

Risk shook his head. "I've never considered making them to sell, but you can find them at Baptiste's Voodoo Shop in the Quarter. They won't be exactly the same as this one, but they'll still have magic."

Landry blinked, unsure of how to react. He didn't think handing out voodoo to kids would go over well. He didn't want to say as much and offend anyone.

Tamil spoke up, sounding unsure if Landry would bite him. "I could probably make a few for you, if you'd like? Baptiste has been teaching me how."

Landry couldn't turn down such a sweet offer.

"I'd love that. Thank you. Just let me know how much I owe you."

Confusion etched Tamil's features. "I don't understand."

Risk rubbed his husband's back. "I think what Tamil means is, he was offering to help you free of charge."

Tamil's confusion didn't fade, but he nodded. "I want to help."

"Okay," Landry said, keeping a smile carefully in place. "I really appreciate it." Damn it. He wanted to know Tamil's story.

Evan moved to his side, saving Landry from making a fool of himself, asking, "I was thinking, you should drink my potion."

Landry blinked at Evan. "Is that a metaphor for something?"

"You can hold my doll, if you'd like?"

At Tamil's sweet offer, Evan huffed at the man. "You helped make it."

"I know. That's why he probably needs protection." Tamil tried handing the doll to Landry again. He was too fascinated to reach for it.

Evan didn't back down. "Well, Saber drank some earlier, and he didn't die."

"He can't die, now can he?" Tamil shot back.

As Landry's gaze swung between the two, trying to follow along with their nonsensical conversation, Baptiste appeared. "Let's all go together. I need to check your work anyhow."

Landry found himself swept along in the tide as they headed for a cauldron. An actual fucking cauldron. Landry couldn't look away. Baptiste used a ladle to scoop up some of the liquid from inside. He sniffed it. "It's missing something. Did you add the kiss for luck? That's the most important ingredient."

Tamil nodded. "We each kissed a side of the rose and tossed it in."

Baptiste shook his head. "It only takes one petal, but you need a real kiss. Here." A rose appeared in Baptiste's hand—like a magician. Landry was mesmerized. Baptiste tore off one petal and handed the rest of the rose to Tamil. "Watch," he said, as if teaching a class. He placed the petal on his bottom lip. Before Landry could guess his next move, Baptiste snagged Evan by the back of the neck and hauled him forward. Their lips met. Landry was transfixed and starting to wonder if he should've paid a fee at the door for all the blatantly sexual shows he was seeing. They weren't even a couple and their kiss was smoking.

"Is this an orgy?" The question popped out before Landry could stop it. "This is an orgy, isn't it?"

The huge Scot with amethyst eyes draped a heavy arm over Landry's shoulders and eyed the kissing pair. "Nay. Sorry. We only have those once a year, and usually in August."

Before Landry could decide if he was joking, Baptiste pulled away and peeled the petal from his lip. "And a kiss for luck," he said, dropping the petal in the cauldron. A tendril of smoke rose from the pot. "There. Perfect. Now you can drink it."

"Is it poisonous?" Landry didn't think anyone here would try to kill him, but he also didn't think people ate rose petals.

"It's perfectly safe," Baptiste said, sounding confident. "It's a draught for luck."

Tamil's gaze swung toward something behind Landry. "Jonathan is coming. Quick, take a swig."

Even though Landry was confused as hell, he accepted a drink from the ladle. It tasted like he'd been mowing, and grass flew in his mouth.

"*Oooh*, is this Tamil and Evan's potion? I want to try."

As the words sounded behind him, Landry turned, and his gaze landed on the center of a man's bare chest. He tilted his chin up to meet the man's stare. He glowed like the sun. His eyes were golden and swirled. He looked jovial, but he had imposing black wings that draped to the ground. Landry blinked, trying to make the image change, but the man was still there. He wore nothing but a kilt. Two beautiful men flanked the angel. He had to be an angel. Landry couldn't think of a better description.

"Did y'all drug me?"

"Why? Are you seeing two of me?" the angel asked, sounding curious.

"Am I dead?"

The angel pinched him. "No. You're alive. It's Landry, right?"

Landry rubbed the spot where Jonathan pinched him and nodded.

"I'm Jonathan," the angel said, holding out his hand.

Landry accepted his handshake. "Y'all drugged me," Landry repeated. There was no other explanation. Jonathan was very real. They were standing too close for Landry to believe anything else. "You have wings."

Jonathan nodded. "Please don't ask to touch them. That's something reserved for my mates."

"I've touched them," Dougal said with a low chuckle that sounded sexual. The comment had

Landry tearing his gaze away from Jonathan. He eyed all the people standing around. They looked expectant, as if awaiting his reaction. Saber stood off to the side, alone, and worrying at his bottom lip.

Landry focused on Jonathan once more. "What's going on?"

Jonathan's smile brightened. "We're having a party, and we've invited you so we can get to know Saber's fated mate."

Landry couldn't even blink. "I'm sorry. What?"

Jonathan's chest expanded as he took a deep breath. "You see, Goddess Celeste—that's who you know as God—she picks one person for every immortal. Their other half. That's who you spend forever with. Well, sometimes you get two people, as you can see from some of the pairings here. It's unavoidable. This is your fate. You were meant to love Saber, and he was meant to love you."

"Is this a cult? I'm in a cult right now, aren't I?"

Jonathan shook his head. He tapped his chest. "I'm a Nephilim. Also the king, but that's another story."

"I'm a wolf," Evan interjected, sounding chipper. When Landry's gaze swung Evan's way, he nodded, as if Landry asked a question. "See." That was all the warning Landry got before Evan pulled his shirt up and over his head. As his hands went to the button on his jeans, Landry's gaze immediately followed. He'd been drugged. Seriously. It was the only explanation. Evan toed off his shoes and took off his pants. Landry couldn't stop staring or blinking like an idiot. The instant he was nude, Evan disappeared. In his place was a large, black wolf. Landry lost the ability to blink. His eyes burned in their need for moisture. For reasons he couldn't explain, Landry sought Tamil with his gaze. Maybe he needed that doll after all.

A sweet smile passed over Tamil's features. He ran his fingers through Evan's fur. Evan's eyes fell closed, and he pressed closer to Tamil's legs. "I can be a wolf too," Tamil said as he pet Evan. "Or anything, really. What would you like? Oh," he said before Landry could respond. "I'm best at being a bird." He looked thoughtful for a moment. "There are lots of birds in Hell for some reason."

"I have to go." The words were out before Landry knew how he'd respond. There were only two possibilities. Either he'd been drugged or these people were some sort of magician side-show cult. Neither choice set well with him.

Faolan tried stopping him. "You cannae leave."

"Let him go," Jonathan said, interceding. "He

needs some time to digest. Saber will go with him." Their words faded away as Landry headed for the house. All he had to do was make it to his car.

"Landry, hold up, sexy. Please?"

At Saber's plea, Landry spun on him in the driveway. "What, Saber? Do you want to tell me you're a wolf too? What the fuck is even happening here?"

Saber's shoulders fell. "I'm not a wolf." Before Landry had time to experience an ounce of relief for a smidge of sanity returning, Saber killed it. "I'm a tiger."

Everything inside Landry froze with horror. Here he was, ninety-eight percent certain he was in love with Saber, and Saber was nuts. That figured. "A tiger," Landry repeated. His voice sounded dead, even to him.

Saber nodded, looking defeated. "That's the real reason I've been running away. I've already ripped up your sheets trying to stop myself from shifting when I lose control with you." He shook his head. "I didn't know how to tell you, Landry."

The image of Landry's sheets floated through his mind. They had looked exactly like a set of sharp claws had swiped through them, cutting them like butter. Landry's heart sped. He couldn't deny the sight of Evan becoming a wolf, or Jonathan as whatever he was. Each breath Landry took came harder than the last. These people, they weren't people. They were animals. Landry bent at the waist and clung to his knees, sucking air. They'd almost made love. He'd definitely done other things—sexual things—with an animal. Landry had to get out of there. He couldn't deal. His stomach churned. This had to be a trippy dream, or a hallucination from the drink they'd given him. Either way, he had to get out of there. These people... He had to go.

"I'm sorry." It was all Landry could squeeze past his tight throat. Saber didn't try stopping him again as he blindly made his way to his SUV. The man who'd stolen him wasn't a man. Landry didn't have the mental capacity to deal with that detail. They were really over. Everything was over.

EIGHT

LANDRY WORKED SO MUCH HE DIDN'T HAVE A ton of friends, and there wasn't a single damn person he could go to with this. The only person he could think to call was Shepherd. Thankfully, his brother answered on the second ring.

"Baby brother."

Landry smiled at Shepherd's greeting. Just hearing his brother's voice made Landry feel better. "Hey. I wondered if you could spare a few minutes for me today—grab a coffee or something. I could use some advice."

"Sure. Can you meet me at Raff's?"

A groan rose in Landry's throat. "Could we meet somewhere else?"

A moment of silence followed his question.

When Shepherd spoke again, he sounded reluctant. "Um, well, I'm already at Raff's. If you want to wait for another day, we can. Otherwise, it'll have to be here."

Landry glanced at his watch. It was two in the afternoon. Apparently, Shepherd had taken up day drinking. It couldn't wait. He needed to figure out his life before he went insane. All Landry could do was hope Saber wasn't there. "All right. Give me half an hour, and I'll be there."

"See you then."

Landry nodded, even though Shepherd couldn't see him. "Yeah. See you then." Landry shoved his phone in his pocket and rubbed his chest. Ever since driving away from Saber, Landry couldn't assuage the empty chasm inside him. He headed for the door, grabbing his keys along the way. Landry drew up short as the door swung wide. Tamil stood there with his hand lifted as if getting ready to knock. He jumped backward when he spotted Landry.

"Sorry," Tamil squeaked, as if he'd done something wrong.

Landry scrambled to soothe him. "Tamil. Hi. Sorry. I wasn't expecting anyone to be standing here." He pasted on a smile. "What brings you by?" Landry tried sneaking a glance around, searching for the man's husband. He couldn't imagine Risk letting Tamil out by himself. Surely Tamil wasn't a prisoner. He just didn't seem brave enough to venture out alone.

"I'm alone," Tamil said, calling Landry out for his search.

Landry's gaze jumped back to his. "Would you like to come in?"

Tamil eyed the space behind him. "No, thank you. Is it okay if we talk out here?"

With a nod, Landry stepped outside and pulled the door closed behind him. He'd do anything Tamil needed to feel safe. No doubt the man learned a hard lesson already about stepping into a stranger's home. Landry motioned toward a set of rocking chairs on the porch. "Have a seat."

Tamil scurried to the chair without taking his eyes off Landry. The move proved he didn't turn his back on strangers. Landry fought the urge to rub his chest again. Tamil's past couldn't be more obviously ugly. Once he was seated, Tamil twisted at the hem of his shirt, looking uncomfortable as hell. "You ran away last night. I worried a lot after you left. I know what it's like to be cast into an environment you don't understand. It bothers me that you might be afraid of us."

"I'm not afraid. At least, I don't think I am." Landry scrubbed at his forehead. "I don't know. It's not that I think you'll hurt me." Landry didn't know how to put his thoughts into words.

Tamil's expression screamed understanding. "The world is bigger than you thought. That's a lot to swallow for someone who sees things in black and white, but everyone you met last night are good people. I was scared too when I first met them. For different reasons, of course. I'd never met anyone nice before Jonathan brought me to live with him. There are still days when I don't handle life well, but you have an advantage over me. You get to walk into this normal."

"Do I?" Landry asked with a chuckle. "Most normal people don't have sex with animals."

A snort escaped Tamil and he covered his mouth to hide the sound. The sight caused a smile to pull at Landry's lips. Tamil dropped his hand and flashed Landry a smile. "Is that what's freaking you out? If so, I think you're seeing things backward. You didn't meet a tiger and fall in love, did you?"

In truth, Landry didn't know how to answer that. So he went with the basics. "No. Until last night, Saber was only a man."

Tamil shrugged. "See? Nothing has changed but

the voice in your head. Don't listen to that. Trust me. I'd go crazy if I didn't wake up every day determined not to hear what my mind whispers." Tamil's expression turned sad. "Of course, you're not crazy like me. Without Risk..." Tamil shook his head and tried for a smile.

Landry fought the urge to comfort him. No doubt Tamil would freak if Landry touched him. "How did you get here? Do you need a lift home?"

"No. I can go wherever I want with a thought, thanks to touching Jonathan. Oh," he said before Landry could wrap his mind around that tidbit. Tamil reached beneath his shirt and pulled out a doll in a yellow dress. "I made this for you. Like I said, I stayed up last night, worrying you hate us. She might not be very good, but I tried."

Landry accepted the doll. The instant he touched her, calm settled over him. He'd never felt so much peace. She wasn't made of much other than burlap and bandages, but Landry instantly adored her. A lump formed in Landry's throat. Tamil's kindness was beyond anything he'd ever encountered. "Thank you. I think this is possibly the nicest thing anyone has ever done for me."

Tamil looked uncomfortable, but a genuine smile still curved his lips. He shrugged and stood. Landry followed his lead. "I hope you'll come see me." He looked everywhere but directly at Landry. "Once Evan goes back to working every day, I probably won't get visitors anymore. Most people aren't like Evan. They're uncomfortable around me, so sorry about that."

"I'm not uncomfortable," Landry rushed to assure him. "You're very sweet. I'm glad we met."

Tamil met his gaze. It was like Landry was staring at a stranger. All innocence was gone. "I'm not sweet. I'm damaged. There's a huge difference between the two. You're a tiger's mate. That makes you stronger than most. I know you don't see it now, but you're blessed. Not everyone gets to know what it's like to not be at everyone else's mercy." Tamil blinked, and he was the meek one again. "Besides, you need to tame Saber so he'll stop being such a tomcat."

A bark of laughter escaped Landry before he realized it would happen. In one statement, Tamil reminded Landry of the real Saber. The guy who drove Landry crazy with his flirting. "Thank you for everything," Landry said, clutching the doll against his chest without realizing it. "I'll keep everything you've said in mind and I'll definitely come visit."

With a shy-looking wave, Tamil disappeared. It

was instant. One second, he was there. The next, he was gone. Landry shook his head. He headed for his SUV, trying not to freak out. There was this huge part of him that couldn't stop wondering if he'd suffered a psychotic break. That was the biggest reason he needed to see his brother. His brother was the stable one. He'd know what to do. It was the first time in Landry's life he was glad Shepherd still saw him as the baby brother. Landry needed an adultier adult. The drive to Raff's passed in a blur, making Landry wonder how he got there without killing anyone. His mind whirled, picking through every minute he'd spent with Saber. How could one person make him feel so alive? How could one person make it so hard to walk away?

Landry's gaze skimmed the parking lot. Shepherd's truck was parked near the dumpster. There were a dozen other cars and two motorcycles, but none of them belonged to Saber. Landry ignored the hint of disappointment that sneaked in. He didn't want to see Saber. Not yet. Maybe not ever. Maybe. Landry scrubbed his hands through his hair. He wanted to see Saber. More than that, he wanted to touch him. Kiss him. Landry wanted everything, but Saber wasn't human. That made Landry wrong for those feelings. Right? Goddamn it. Tamil was right. Everything had been black and white before Saber. Now, he didn't know anymore.

With a growl, Landry threw open his car door and headed for the building. He searched the tables with his gaze for any sign of Shepherd.

"Yo, baby brother."

Landry followed the sound of his brother's shouted words. He was behind the bar, wearing an apron. Landry's eyebrows rose at the sight. He headed Shepherd's way. "What's this?" he asked, claiming the first stool he came to.

Shepherd winked and went back to slicing lemons and limes. "I got laid off."

"What?" Landry recognized that he damn near shrieked the word. He lowered his voice. "You just got promoted. I mean, what the hell?"

"Just one of those things," Shepherd said with a shrug. He'd always been an unfailingly positive person. "The call came down from corporate. My whole line got the ax. They say it's temporary, but who knows. Anyhow, Raff gave me a job until..." He shrugged again. "Whenever."

Landry forgot his problems. "Are you making that two-hour drive to work every day?"

Landry shook his head. "I have to let my apartment go. This pays more than unemployment but way less than what I made. Not to mention, making the drive would be hell on my old truck. Raff said I can stay with Dante and him until I find something closer."

It was obvious Raff was a godsend but still. "Why didn't you call me? I have a spare room."

A humorless laugh escaped Shepherd. "Pride, baby brother. Pride. Your life is always so." He waved the knife around as if searching for his words. "Put together," he said finally. He flashed Landry a sad smile. "You haven't married the wrong person or been divorced. If anyone has ever cheated on you, you've never said. Hell, I'm not sure you've ever been in love, much less let anyone break you. You've worked the same job since forever." He shook his head. It was the first time Landry had ever heard Shepherd sound bitter. "You've always known yourself, gone for whatever you want, and never failed. That's not me, Landry. Not only do I not know myself at all, I fail at everything. Something is just... missing, I guess."

Landry didn't know what to say. He'd never suspected his brother felt like he couldn't talk to him. Landry wasn't perfect. That wasn't it at all. Everything Shepherd listed was true or had been true before Saber. Before Saber, Landry had never taken a single risk. Not really. He always played things safe. Landry told himself it was the smart way to live. In truth, he'd been waiting for something more. Something bigger. He'd been waiting for Saber.

"Hey, Shep. Do you—"

Shepherd jumped and spun as Raff appeared at his back. Raff leapt backward, trying to avoid the blade in Shepherd's hand. It sliced through Raff's shirt.

"Oh my god, Raff. I'm so sorry. How bad is it? Do I need to call 911? Maybe Landry has his radio."

Raff clasped the edge of the counter. His chest heaved as if he'd run a mile. A low chuckle escaped the overly large bar owner. "You didn't get me. Don't worry. You just ruined my shirt."

Landry and Shepherd both dropped their chins and eyed the black t-shirt that stretched across the man's barrel chest before turning baggy at his trim waist. There was an obvious sliced hole across his side.

Shepherd set the knife aside. "Jesus Christ, Raff. Are you sure? I'm such a fucking idiot."

Dante sidled up next to Raff. "Is everything okay?"

Raff smiled, showing off a set of gorgeous

dimples and straight, white teeth. "Everything is fine. Shepherd put a nice-sized hole in my shirt but missed my precious hide."

Shepherd swiped a hand across his eyes. "I'm so fucking sorry. It's like I can't stop fucking up everything I touch."

"I promise I'm good," Raff said, warming Landry's heart with his caring tone and obvious concern over Shepherd's feelings. He rolled his shirt up, showing off a set of hairy and delicious abs. He held Shepherd's stare. "See? It's all good. I've got a thousand of these bar logo shirts. Don't worry, okay?"

Shepherd never lifted his chin. It was obvious he couldn't look away. "It's a damn good thing, since it looks like you've already been stabbed in the same spot once before."

Raff's smile fell. "What?" He dropped his gaze to his stomach. Landry did too. The same place Shepherd had sliced Raff's shirt, there was a ragged-looking scar—like someone had slashed him with a knife. Raff's chin jerked up. His gaze sought Dante's. For a full minute, they stared at one another. Landry had no idea what the problem was, but he swore he felt something break.

Dante shook his head. He visibly swallowed, looking like he'd been punched in the throat. "I..."

He turned and walked away, heading for the door without finishing his sentence.

Raff stared after him, looking every bit as devastated. "Fuck me," Raff growled, going after him.

Shepherd's gaze swung Landry's way. "What the hell?"

Landry cast a look around, searching for anything to say. He was as lost as Shepherd. His gaze landed on a lone figure, sitting in the corner, drinking a beer, and staring out the window. How Landry had missed Saber's presence was beyond him. Now that he'd seen him, Landry couldn't look away. Longing like he'd never experienced punched him in the gut. Shepherd's claims overwhelmed him again. He'd never taken a real chance in his life. Fuck what everyone else thought. Nothing had felt wrong with Saber.

"I'm sorry, Landry. I know you came to talk." Landry tore his eyes away from Saber and focused on Shepherd. His brother looked upset and ready to bolt. His gaze stayed locked on the door Dante and Raff had disappeared through. "I need to check on them." He turned to a nearby waitress. "Could you watch the bar for a minute?"

She nodded.

Landry waved him away. "Go. Do what you need to do. We'll talk later."

Shepherd looked distracted but gave him a sharp nod, acknowledging Landry's words as he headed for the door. Landry didn't watch him go. Instead, his feet moved in Saber's direction with no real plan in mind. It was like there was a magnet inside his chest, pulling him across the room to his polar opposite. The second he reached Saber's side, his palm slid across Saber's shoulder and stayed. He felt warm and touching Saber soothed something inside Landry.

Saber glanced up and held his stare. He looked hurt—like Landry's leaving had wounded him deeply. Landry didn't speak. He didn't know what to say. All he knew was, he couldn't drag his hand away. Only when they were connected did he feel whole. Saber had taken a huge risk on him. That detail hadn't occurred to Landry until now. Saber's secret was bigger than anything Landry had ever encountered. His safety depended on no one ever knowing. Landry imagined—if anyone knew—Saber would be dissected like an animal. He didn't know how big their world was or how many others were out there, but Saber wasn't safe as long as anyone knew. Yet he'd told Landry, knowing the risks. Landry had immediately proven he wasn't worth it.

Saber covered Landry's hand and lifted it to his mouth. His lips skimmed the back. For a moment, he held Landry there. His eyes fell closed. Landry's filled with tears. He blinked them away. Landry couldn't walk away without knowing he'd faced this with everything he had. He cleared his throat, trying to speak past the lump forming there.

"Would you show me?"

Saber turned his head and rested his warm cheek on Landry's hand. He nodded. "If you'd like."

Landry cleared his throat again, praying he wouldn't choke. "I think I have to see."

After pushing his chair from the table, Saber stood. He didn't release Landry's hand as they headed for the door. "You'll have to drive. I came on foot." That seemed like a long-ass walk to Landry, but he didn't say as much. A soft chuckle escaped Saber. "Tigers can run up to forty miles an hour. The pool hall is on Raff's property, which backs up to mine. He doesn't care if I cut through."

"It's like you can read my mind sometimes," Landry said with a shake of his head. Saber cast him a closed glance, and Landry knew. Saber could hear his thoughts. Landry swallowed as he climbed inside his SUV. He tried hard not to flip out. "So Raff knows about you?"

Saber buckled his seat belt as he answered. "Yes." He met Landry's gaze, looking serious. "You're in Were country, baby."

In a last-ditch effort to stay calm, Landry concentrated on pulling out from the lot. "Does that mean Raff is a tiger too?" That didn't sound like something Shepherd could handle.

"No." Before Landry could sigh with relief, Saber killed it. "He's a wolf like Evan. The alpha of the southeast pack, to be specific. No one stays here without his permission."

One issue at a time. Landry could only deal with so much. "Oh." Honestly, he had nothing else. By the time they reached Saber's cabin, Landry's insides shook. It was one thing to see a stranger turn into a wolf. The idea of seeing Saber become a tiger scared the fuck out of him.

"You don't have to do this," Saber said, cutting through Landry's panic. "You can walk away from me and never look back."

That wasn't true in the least. Landry couldn't unlearn any of this. More than that, he couldn't walk away from Saber without trying. "No. I can't." He leapt from the car without further explanation. Saber had already proven he could see Landry's thoughts. The guy knew Landry couldn't back down now. "Where are we doing this?"

"Right here, I guess," Saber said. He swiped his hands down his thighs, looking nervous. "That way, you can jump back in your car and leave, if you want." Saber winced, as if saying the words hurt.

Landry nodded and leaned against the driver's side door. He crossed his arms over his chest, trying to hide the way his hands shook. With a sharp nod, Saber pulled his shirt up and over his head before toeing off his boots. Landry took a deep breath. His nervousness dimmed. Goddamn, Saber was beautiful. That wide chest and solid muscle, fuck. Saber's hands went for the button on his jeans. Landry's gaze dropped, refusing to miss a single moment. He slid his zipper down, revealing a trail of dark blond hair. Landry's heart sped. He wasn't sure he cared what happened next any longer as long as Saber kept stripping. Saber peeled off his jeans. He stood proud in his nudity as he should. Landry could barely breathe past his swollen tongue. No one compared to Saber—not physically and not in the way he made Landry feel.

"You can still stop me."

Landry met Saber's gaze. Those blue eyes owned him. "Don't stop." Even Landry heard the breathless note to his voice. He didn't care. There was no turning back.

Saber gave him a sharp nod. It happened fast. One second, he'd been staring at Saber. The next, a huge tiger paced in front of him. There been no popping of bones and painful transformation like in the movies. It just happened. Landry straightened away from the SUV. Saber was a white tiger. The eyes were the same. Landry hadn't expected either of those things. He couldn't move. All Landry could do was stare. He'd never seen a tiger in real life. They had them at the zoo, but Landry had never seen them. Not to mention, being this close was surreal as fuck. Saber inched closer. A small, sane part of Landry recognized he should be scared. He wasn't. His hand lifted without thought. Saber dipped his head beneath his palm, like a giant cat petting himself. His eyes fell closed as Landry rubbed him. His fur was soft in some spots and rough in others. Landry lost himself in the discovery.

You're so brave.

Landry froze as Saber's voice filled his head. He didn't think he was crazy. He'd heard him. Testing his theory, Landry answered aloud, "I'm not sure it's bravery driving me right now."

Then what is?

Landry sucked in a breath. He worried he was one discovery more away from mentally breaking. Still, it was Saber, and Landry couldn't help the way he felt. Landry eyed the tiger that could kill him in one strike. It didn't feel like he was standing there with a tiger. He was there with Saber. Landry couldn't lie to himself and he couldn't lie to Saber. He was there for Saber. Everything else was secondary. "Love is driving me," he admitted, because he had to, or the weight would kill him. "I'm not brave. This isn't something I feel like I can handle, but I have to anyway, because I love you."

Saber was a man again, standing inches away and holding Landry's stare. "Tell me how to make this easier," Saber begged, sounding willing to do anything. "If you tell me you never want to see me in tiger form again, I'll never change in your presence. We can pretend I'm normal."

A sharp pain stabbed Landry through the heart. Saber's mouth said he was willing, but Landry felt the truth. He felt the way Landry's rejection of his true nature would wound him. If Landry said he couldn't handle Saber as is, Saber would try to be different, but they'd both always know Landry had rejected part of him. Landry took another deep breath. His hands found Saber's waist. "I want all of you." As the words left his lips, the truth settled into his gut. He really did. Landry wanted Saber—scary bits and all. He didn't know what that entailed and not knowing terrified him, but fuck all. Landry wanted him.

Saber didn't look happy or triumphant. Instead, he looked possessive and hungry, which was so much better. Butterflies stirred in Landry's stomach. "If you choose me, there's more to it than simply saying you want me."

Of course, there was, because life. Landry licked his lips, feeling his nerves grow again. "Okay."

"I'll bite you."

To his surprise, Landry's knees weakened. His cock jerked. "Okay." Damn, even Landry heard how breathless he sounded.

"And you'll bite me."

Yeah, he would. The phantom sensation of sinking his teeth into Saber's skin made Landry's teeth itch with desire. "Anything else?"

Saber gave him a sharp nod. "The bite marks will scar. Any Were who sees you will recognize you're mated."

Landry's brows pulled together. Things were getting deep. He wanted it that way, but he didn't one hundred percent understand. "Mated?"

"It would be like we're married, except it can't be broken. Being with me is for life, and life is a very long time. I'm immortal. Even though I can die, I'm not easy to kill."

Doubt crept in. Landry wouldn't live forever. His hands fell away. "I..." Goddamn, he felt like a failure. Emotion choked him. Saber deserved someone who wouldn't grow old.

"There's more."

A humorless laugh escaped Landry. "All right."

"Once we're mated, your life will be tied to mine. Weres are ruled by Norse gods, which means mates live and die together. If I live another thousand years, you will too."

"And if you die?"

"Age will catch up with you," Saber said, dropping the truth on him.

Landry stepped around Saber and headed for the cabin. He made it to the door before he realized Saber hadn't followed. Landry turned and met Saber's gaze. He looked worried and unsure of what move to make. Landry motioned for Saber to follow. "I don't really want to do this outside."

Still, Saber didn't immediately move. "Are you being serious?"

Landry was terrified to his core, but he'd never

been more serious. "Saber, move your ass, or I will get started without you."

Saber was behind him in a flash, herding Landry inside. He was large and overwhelming. Landry wanted to laugh at Saber's enthusiasm, but no sound would pass his throat. He felt like he'd been waiting for Saber forever. Realistically, Landry knew that wasn't true. It had never been like this for him. The ache. The yearning. Everything inside Landry cried out for Saber. His cells were on high alert, anticipating something monumental, even though Landry didn't know what.

Landry made it as far as the center of the living room. An animalistic sound he'd never heard filled the air a half second before Landry hit the floor. It didn't hurt. Saber braced his fall, but Landry couldn't move. Saber's massive weight pinned him to the floor. His clothes ripped away. The sound of material tearing mixed with Landry's gasps for air. Saber kissed every newly bared inch of skin. Landry caught himself humping the floor, seeking relief for his leaking cock. Each time Saber's teeth scraped his skin, a moan vibrated from Landry's throat. His balls were already tight. One of Saber's large fingers probed at his hole. Landry tried digging his fingernails into the wood floor. He sucked air. Something even larger pushed against his asshole.

"Condom," Landry yelled, trying to hang on to sanity.

A sexy chuckle sounded behind him. "I can't get or spread disease."

There was that. Saber tried again to push his way inside. Landry sucked in a hiss. "Lube," he reminded Saber, wondering if Saber had completely lost his senses.

Saber froze behind him. "Um, shit. I don't think I have anything like that."

Landry pressed his forehead to the floor. Things continued piling on. It was like they weren't meant to ever have sex. Aggravation owned Landry. He'd been craving Saber for so long. Landry took a deep breath. "I guess this isn't happening, then."

Saber kissed him between the shoulder blades. "I'm sorry. That's just not something I considered."

All Landry could do was laugh. "It figures your kind wouldn't need something like that."

"Yeah, um, that's probably not true. I wouldn't know."

Landry's brain froze. "Okay," he said, dragging out the word. "What?"

Saber's lips brushed the back of Landry's neck,

doing nothing to cool the situation. His mouth moved to Landry's ear. He licked the shell. "I've never actually had sex with a man before."

"I'm sorry. What?"

Saber went still at the question as if defeated.

Landry didn't know why he had such a hard time wrapping his brain around the situation, but there it was. He'd come to terms with Saber being a tiger, but being his first man, that stumped him. He floundered for a moment. They couldn't do this. Not like this anyhow. Saber's confession made Landry realize something. He wasn't the only one in new waters. Learning Saber wasn't human had thrown him, but at least Saber looked human and Landry could pretend. He couldn't imagine being gay his entire life and suddenly he couldn't resist a woman. Landry would be terrified. Saber hadn't seemed bothered, but he also wasn't the type to show it. No wonder he kept running away.

"Okay. I've got this." Landry wasn't sure if he was talking to Saber or himself. "Let me up." He could feel Saber's defeat as he rolled away. It was like a physical touch pressing on his brain. Landry did his best not to make things weird. Nude and hard, Landry headed for the kitchen. Even he couldn't believe he was doing this, but desperate times. Not to mention, Saber needed him. Landry could feel it. Nothing mattered more than making Saber happy. Thankfully, he found what he needed right away. Back in the living room, he found Saber still sprawled on the floor with his fingers linked behind his head. He stared at the ceiling as if trying to squelch the misery. Landry stole a moment to enjoy his beauty. Large, hard, and blond all over, Saber was the most beautiful man Landry had ever seen. He was masculine perfection. Long legs. Bulging muscles. Thick cock. Landry's mouth watered.

"Bedroom," Landry demanded, shaking the bottle of coconut oil at Saber.

Saber's eyes lit. He scrambled to his feet. With a smirk, Landry headed through the only other door. A large bed took up the center of the room. He spotted the bathroom through a door inside the bedroom. The cabin was small and intimate. Landry liked it a lot. That was probably because Saber lived there, and Landry was completely in love with him.

Landry pointed toward the bed. "On your back."

Saber's eyebrows rose, as if he planned to argue.

Landry cut him off. "Nope. On your back. I get that you're used to being in charge and you'll probably snap soon, but right this moment, you're following orders."

The way Saber smirked as he made a show of settling onto his back let Landry know he wouldn't obey for long. That was fine, but Landry was the expert in the room right now. Landry leaned over and kissed Saber's stomach. Saber's fingers immediately found Landry's hair and held on, making his scalp sting. He kept Saber distracted by licking his abs while he opened the oil. Landry set one knee on the bed and moved lower. His lips skimmed Saber's soaked crown. Saber's hips left the mattress. Landry's tongue shot out. He needed to taste Saber's cum. The salty juices coating Saber's crown filled Saber's mouth. His eyes fell closed. Damn. His cock jumped. There was no patience left in him. He fisted Saber's dick, making it shine with oil, before tossing his leg over Saber's body and straddling him. As he claimed Saber's lips, Landry reached down and toyed with his own asshole, coating himself with oil. Not only was Saber large, he was also inexperienced with men. Landry didn't want to get hurt. Neither could he wait for Saber to get anything more than a crash course.

He held Saber's bottom lip between his teeth and positioned Saber's cock. Landry pressed down, impaling himself. He gasped. His dick jerked, dripping more pre-cum onto Saber's stomach. The moment he was fully seated, Saber rolled. With one of Landry's knees draped over Saber's arm and the man's tongue filling his mouth, Saber rocked. A deep moan vibrated through Landry. Saber hit at the perfect angle. Landry couldn't think straight. There were too many thoughts in his head at one time—like Saber's were overwhelming him.

You feel too good, Landry. I can't fight it.

Landry held his breath. He wasn't imagining things. He could hear Saber inside his head. Feel the man's pleasure. It mixed with his, making Landry insane. Pressure beat at his crown, trying to break free. His gums itched like he was having an allergic reaction. He wanted to bury his teeth into something hard and make it stop.

Please don't freak out and push me away. I can't stop it.

Landry was too close and too agitated to question Saber's panicked thoughts. Saber threw his head back and sucked air as he pumped inside Landry. The sexy sight only made Landry's skin tighter. As Landry looked on, Saber's features changed, becoming flatter and more animal-like.

Bite me, Landry. Give in. I can't hold back much longer.

With no real plan in mind, and going on pure

instinct, Landry tugged Saber down. Their bodies went flush. Saber's abs massaged at Landry's hard cock with each push inside Landry's ass. Pleasure owned him. Madness controlled him. The itching worsened in Landry's gums. He sank his teeth into Saber's neck. They sliced through the skin easily, puncturing like they'd magically sharpened. Blood filled Landry's mouth. He should've been disgusted. Instead, he swallowed like it was Saber's cum. An orgasm ripped through him, stealing all his senses. Ecstasy clouded everything. A roar filled the air— like a tiger tearing into its prey. Another wave of pleasure rocked him to his core. Saber held him down and tore into his throat. There was a split second of excruciating pain before he nearly blacked out from the elation. His cock wouldn't stop jerking and emptying his balls. He felt Saber's orgasm as if it was his, and there was a tugging at his chest. It felt like he was being physically stitched together with Saber, making them one. He'd never been so overwhelmed. The world around them ceased to exist. Their mouth clashed, sucking and licking. A copper tang joined with Saber's usual flavor. Landry felt complete. He didn't ever want to move or stop.

I love you.

Landry's eyes unexpectedly filled with tears as the words brushed his brain in a loving caress.

I promise I'll always protect you.

Landry's throat tightened. Saber's thoughts felt like wedding vows. Landry had never wanted something so badly in his life. Saber meant everything to him. Walking away from all he'd ever known had never been so easy.

"I love you." Landry needed to say the words aloud, so Saber couldn't doubt they came from him.

Saber lightly brushed his lips across Landry's. "I love you too. Stay with me."

A tired-sounding chuckle escaped Landry. "I couldn't move right now if I wanted to."

"For good," Saber clarified. He kept stealing tiny kisses and Landry's heart. "I know this place isn't huge and we'll probably be on top of each other all the time, but stay."

Landry didn't think he had a choice. The moment he'd chosen to get in this bed, he'd chosen a life with Saber. The only reason things were complicated at all was because Landry was human. Landry didn't doubt, if he was like Saber, it would be understood that he now lived wherever Saber did. Maybe he wasn't a weretiger, but Landry would do his damnedest to keep things normal for Saber.

"You're mine. I'm not going anywhere. We'll figure out how to combine our stuff and I have zero issues with being on top of you."

Saber's body shook with barely suppressed laughter. He rolled and repositioned their bodies with Landry's back against his chest. On their sides, Saber squeezed Landry against him, hugging him tight. "I was so scared," Saber admitted, sounding lost. "Since the moment we met, I knew you were special, but I never believed you'd accept me. Every time I tried to think of a way to explain, my insides shook with fear. I can't lose you, but I didn't know how to explain this."

A chuckle escaped Landry. It wasn't funny, but he was ecstatic, and it kept bursting from him in waves. He tried calming his still racing heart. Saber needed his assurances right now. "Maybe springing your friends on me wasn't the best choice."

"That's probably true," Saber said, kissing his neck. "But I didn't think turning tiger or just telling you was the best either."

That was true. If he'd turned into a tiger, Landry would've probably had himself committed. On the other hand, if Saber had made the claim without proof, Landry would've driven him straight to the mental ward. In truth, there'd been no good way to handle it. "None of that matters. I've had my time to process. Now all I want is this," Landry said, snuggling closer. Saber kept licking Landry's shoulder and neck where he'd bitten him. Landry would've thought something like that would weird him out. In truth, he was having a hard time breathing properly or thinking about anything else. He reached over his head and buried his fingers in Saber's hair, holding him in place. Another thought hit him.

"Eventually, people will wonder why I'm not getting older."

Saber froze with his lips pressed to Landry's neck. "Yes. Eventually, you'll have to leave your job. I'm sorry. I guess I should've given you more time and information. That's why everyone sticks to our little town right here. Otherwise, it gets hard to explain why you're not aging."

He was having a hard time finding any regret in his heart. "Don't stop," Landry begged, already missing the way Saber's tongue felt against his skin. There were too many questions Landry needed answered to worry over it today. Apparently, they had forever. Landry didn't know why he wasn't freaking out. Maybe it was because they were meant to be. There was a higher power involved that saw his life better than Landry ever could. Not to mention, he had Saber's nude body pressing against him. Right now, everything felt a lot like heaven. Landry was home.

SABER COULDN'T STOP KISSING the spot where he'd marked Landry as his. The wound had already healed, leaving a scar behind that would warn all other immortals he was mated. Every Were Landry encountered would avert their eyes, ensuring Saber understood they wouldn't encroach on his mate. This was his other half. The person Goddess Celeste handpicked for him.

His cock was still hard as a rock. He'd gone too long without sex and he couldn't stop wanting it now. His dick was slick with oil and cum. Saber couldn't stop humping Landry's ass like a full-blown pervert. Landry felt too good in his arms. His scent drove Saber insane. Without thought or any real plan in mind, Saber rolled Landry beneath him. With Landry's stomach pressed to the bed and his teeth sunk into Landry's shoulder, Saber easily slipped inside Landry's ass once more. A sharp gasp left Landry's lips.

He backed away. "I'm sorry. Are you sore?"

Landry held tight to his hair. "Don't stop."

At the plea, Saber rolled his hips, moving slow. This time, he made love to Landry. His every movement was calculated and paced. He'd already claimed his mate in a rough and frenzied tumble. This time, it was about assuaging his heart. Saber didn't know if he would've fallen for Landry if they weren't fated, but he believed he would have. Not only did Landry make him happy, Landry possessed a beautiful and forgiving heart. He made Saber want to be a good person. Saber knew being with him wouldn't be easy for Landry. There was a lot Landry would have to give up, eventually. Things would change for him. Yet Landry wasn't freaking or complaining. He was reveling and submitting. That was sexy as hell.

Saber rolled his hips. A low moan rose in his chest as the tugging on his cock won his attention. His mind was linked to Landry's now. He could hear his thoughts. Feel what he felt. Saber used the connection to his advantage, pushing Landry closer to the edge. He could make Landry come like this—with just their connection. Saber intended to do just that. He wanted to prove he could keep his mate satisfied. Always. Saber closed his eyes and concentrated on Landry. He pictured his tongue lapping at Landry's cock, as he'd done the day he'd almost broke tiger on him. Landry writhed against the mattress, openly seeking more. Saber held on and gave him everything. When Landry's orgasm hit, it stole Saber's. As he cried out and rode each wave, Saber never released his tight hold on Landry. This was his home—inside this man. They would never be broken or parted. Saber had never felt freer or more powerful.

NINE

THE QUARTER WAS HOT AS FUCK IN HIS DARK uniform with the sun bearing down on him and people pressing in. Still, Landry slowed several times when he caught his reflection in shop windows. The scars on his throat were more prevalent than he ever expected. Yet they mesmerized him. It was like a new wedding band. Instead of constantly looking at his hand, Landry kept staring at his neck. Life was surreal.

The past six weeks of being mated to Saber had been amazing. His house had sold faster than anticipated, leaving them very little time to decide how to combine their things. His drive to and from work was way longer than it used to be. It was always a lot quieter at the cabin. In spite of all the adjustments, Landry had no complaints. Well, Saber snored, but Landry had known that already. It was also an adorable sound—like a vibration in his chest. Landry always went out like a light with the sound brushing his ear. A smile pulled at Landry's lips at the thought.

"You look happy." Landry tore his gaze away from his reflection.

Evan had one hand clinging to the door frame of the shop while hanging out the open door. His smile grew once he had Landry's attention. "Awwww, look at those mating marks. That's so sweet."

Landry automatically searched for Evan's. They peeked out above his shirt collar. His gaze skirted away. "What brings you out in this horrible heat?"

Evan straightened and waved Landry inside. "This is where I work. Come in. It's a lot cooler inside."

As Landry followed Evan inside, he caught sight of the name on the door—Baptiste's Voodoo Shop. It was the place Tamil had mentioned. It was low lit and much cooler inside the shop. Baptiste stood behind the counter. He flashed Landry a smile. Dante leaned against the other side of the counter, flipping through a magazine. When he spotted

Landry, his expression closed. He straightened and headed for the back door.

Landry shot Evan a questioning look.

Evan shrugged. "His feelings are hurt. It's not your fault. He's been with Raff for well over fifty years. Even though they both knew Raff would find his fated mate eventually, it still broke him when Shepherd showed up."

For a moment, Landry couldn't think of a response. "What about Shepherd?"

Baptiste and Evan exchanged glances. Evan was the one who answered. "Shepherd is Raff's fated mate. I thought you knew. From what I heard, you were there when Shepherd scarred Raff with that knife. Things turned pretty ugly really fast between Dante and Raff after that."

Shit. Landry hadn't thought of that day again. He shook his head. "I'm an idiot. Everything has kind of been a blur since then. I should probably call and check on that."

Baptiste shrugged. "It's like that when you find your mate. The pull is powerful. It takes over your life. Weres are luckier than Vampires. If one of you dies, the other tends to follow shortly after. Vampires don't. We continue on in an extremely painful existence, never feeling whole again."

Landry tried to show no reaction. It didn't happen. "You're a vampire."

Evan's musical laugh filled the store.

Baptiste's smile looked indulgent. "I'm thinking we should have another get-together at Jonathan's. You have a lot to learn. Your world just became huge, Landry Khatri."

Landry rushed to correct him. "Oh, Saber and I haven't gotten married yet. It's LaTour."

Evan and Baptiste both burst into laughter. Evan apologized as he swiped at his eyes. "You should probably go home and kick Saber's ass. I shouldn't have to be the one to tell you that mark on your neck means you're married. Your last name is now his, since you're now a part of his pack. It's all tied up in the eyes of Goddess Celeste." Evan looked thoughtful. "I guess that makes it a pack of two now since Sierra is gone. Tigers aren't very sociable." He waved toward Baptiste. "Speaking of last names, Baptiste can get you all your paperwork. You'll need him to make everything look legal in the eyes of men. He's also the one who will change things for you throughout the years, making sure your IDs match the age you look."

Baptiste straightened away from the counter. "Thanks for reminding me. Let me see your license."

Half in shock, Landry handed over his wallet. Baptiste flipped through everything. "There," he said, handing it back. "And here," he said, reaching beneath the counter and coming up with some papers. After he passed his hand over them, they transformed into certificates. Landry eyed the contents of his wallet. Everything had changed to Saber's last name. The certificate was his signed and sealed marriage license.

"This doesn't change anything in the world's complex computer system. I doubt any of this would hold up anywhere." At least, that was what Landry told himself to keep from freaking out. However, seeing that marriage certificate did something to his chest. Something he liked a little too much.

Baptiste shrugged. "You have the documentation to back up any claims you make. That's all that matters to any human you meet. They're just working a job. If you say it's true and show them the paperwork, they'll shrug and change your info in their system. Trust me. I'm very old. Some might even say ancient."

Evan jumped in. "I know it's a lot to take in, but you'll learn on the fly. If you ever have any questions, please come see me. I was born a Were, but my family all died when I was really young. There are times when I have to ask about things I should already know. So I'm here. If I don't know, I don't mind embarrassing myself by asking around."

Landry genuinely liked Evan. He was sweet. "Thank you. I'll keep that in mind." He glanced at his watch. "I get off soon, so I should probably go kill Saber for not telling me about this," he said, shaking the papers.

Bleidd appeared through the door Dante had disappeared through. He snagged Evan around the waist from behind and hauled him against his chest. His silver hair was pulled back away from his face. He truly was a good-looking man. He flashed Landry a smile. "Don't kill Saber. Just make him beg a little. Torment is always more enjoyable than murder."

Evan motioned toward Bleidd. "He would know. I stay mad at him a lot." *Not really,* he silently mouthed, making Landry laugh.

"Since I know where you are, I'll stop by more often. I'm on foot patrol in this area at least once a week."

With a final round of goodbyes. Landry headed out, making his way to his car.

Landry glanced down at the papers in his hand. *Saber, I might still kill you.*

What did I do?

Landry stopped in his tracks. It was the first time they'd spoken like this when they weren't together. *You can hear me?*

He felt Saber's mental eye roll. *Of course. What have I done wrong?*

You didn't tell me I have a different last name now.

Oh. Saber sounded so unconcerned, Landry fought a growl. *Sorry. I didn't even think about it. You're my mate. I thought I'd explained that's so much bigger than marriage. Marriage is a human thing. It can end at any time. What we have is forever; even death can't break it. Since I've never been human, it's hard for me to think of everything you need to learn. I can only cross bridges as we come to them.*

That sounded fair. Landry felt a little better after that explanation. *So what are you doing right now?*

I just got home. I'm about to jump in the shower.

Landry unlocked his car and slid behind the wheel. *Wait for me. I'm on my way.*

I don't know. Saber's sultry tone taunted Landry. *I've already got the hot water going. I can practically feel the water streaming down my body already. It'll take you at least twenty minutes to get here. I don't know if I can keep from touching myself that long.*

Landry couldn't stop smiling like an idiot. He was so in love with this gigantic fool who'd stolen him. *So be it.* Landry released an inner sigh. *I guess I'll just pull over right here and pleasure myself since I'm not needed at home.* The animalistic growl that rumbled through his head had Landry biting his lip to keep from laughing.

You're mine. Get home.

At Saber's order, Landry sped up. Saber's world meant keeping secrets and was—most likely— dangerous. There were days when it felt overwhelming. Landry wondered when this new life would bite him in the ass. Right now, though, Landry was the happiest man on the planet. There was nothing that mattered more to him than getting home and taking a shower. Everything else could wait.

Keep an eye out for the next book in the series, Ravage.

Please consider leaving a review at the retailer where this book was purchased. Reviews really help with a book's visibility, which ensures I can continue writing. Thank you, Charity.

ABOUT THE AUTHOR

Charity Parkerson is an award winning and multi-published author with several companies. Born with no filter from her brain to her mouth, she decided to take this odd quirk and insert it in her characters.

*Seven-time Readers' Favorite Award Winner
  *2015 Passionate Plume Award Finalist
  *2013 Reviewers' Choice Award Winner
  *2012 ARRA Finalist for Favorite Paranormal Romance
  *Five-time winner of The Mistress of the Darkpath

Connect with her online:

--Join my street team: facebook.com/TeamCharityParkerson
  --Sign up for my newsletter: http://bit.ly/CharityNews

--Website: charityparkerson.com

--Facebook:

facebook.com/authorCharityParkerson

facebook.com/TheMenofSin

--Twitter: twitter.com/CharityParkerso